WHIMPER WONDERLAND

THE SEEKERS CLUB BOOK #1

ADORA CROOKS

CONTENT INFORMATION

Welcome to The Seekers Club.

This is a spicy, cozy romance that revolves around characters in the kink lifestyle. They often engage in BDSM "play" and power exchange dynamics in the bedroom.

This book is about two people who overcome toxic relationships and reclaim their power through kink.

For the full list of trigger warnings and content, please visit my website.

https://adoracrooksbooks.com

THE SEEKERS

LIST OF MEMBERS

- Dove (Legal Name: Sadie)
- Dorian (Legal Name: Dorian)
- Ophelia (Legal Name: Ruby)
- Carver (Legal Name: Unknown)
- Phantom (Legal Name: Unknown)
- Princess (Legal Name: Unknown)

CHEESE > MEN

Dove. Now.

If this man were a cheese, he'd be brie.

Buttery. Decadent. I'd spread him across the heel of a baguette. I'd suck his white, creamy residue off my thumb. I'd leave no crumbs behind.

Am I being thirsty? Well, maybe, but I've been on a sex-hiatus for nearly a year, and the man cozying up to me at the bar is exactly my type. Handsome in a rough way, with tattoos that run up his arms and curl like smoke up the side of his neck. Probably early-twenties, he's got that fresh-out-of-NYU-scent, which is a little young for me, but beggars can't be choosers.

It's his hands that draw me to him. Corded arms. Fingers with a wide wingspan. Hands that could grab a fistful of my hair or wrap nicely around my throat.

I don't do that anymore, but *I can still dream.*

I'm closing out when Mr. Brie closes the gap between us and fills the space on the stool next to me. I'm in a black dress that's not meant for him, but he's admiring it all the same. His eyes meet mine, and I don't look away, so he smiles and says, "Hey. Can I buy you a drink?"

I check the time on my phone. I have to be across the street in five minutes, where my submissive is waiting for me. Every minute I'm late will just extend his agony, but he is *literally a masochist*, sooo…

"I have somewhere to be," I tell him. "But I can be late."

He's not phased. "Then we'll have to make every minute count, Ms.…" My wallet is sitting on the bar. He pulls it towards him so he can read my ID through the plastic window. "Sadie Royal."

"Wow," I say. "Nosy."

I slip my hand over my wallet, trying to pull it back. My wallet is thick, but only because it's packed with junk —tattoo shop business cards and cafe punch-tickets. He holds tight, keeping his grip on my wallet. He checks it out again, and then his eyes scan my face, like he's looking for some clue hidden there. He asks: "You're thirty-five?"

"I am. What about it?"

A smile quirks the edge of his mouth. He nods sagely, like we've both entered into some secret, private contract. Then he says the worst thing imaginable. "Good for you."

Good for you?

What the ever-loving fuck does *good for you* mean?

It's a real clit-killer and all the single-woman-at-a-bar confidence drains from my body, transfused with a slowly rising rage. I grab my wallet and pocket it, rising from the bar.

"Hey," he says, "what about that drink?"

"Raincheck." I pull on my jacket and don't turn back. That was my resolution this year. *Don't give shitty men the time of day.*

I check my phone. Five past. I'm officially late, and Dorian is officially squirming.

The second I exit the bar, I'm met with a blast of cold air that nearly bites my face off. Winter is New York City is brutal. Dorian's apartment is just down the block, but I have to survive a tunnel of icy wind to get there. I brace myself, buttoning my coat tightly around my middle and donning a traffic-cone orange beanie.

My boots crunch over salt crystals. It snowed yesterday, and what was once white and pretty is now grey and dirty slush lining the streets. I skip over it as I cross the street. I pass by a horror-themed bookstore ("The Paper Cut," with a window display in full, gothic Christmas mode, black tinsel and a decrepit tree) and stop in front of the red door that leads to Dorian's apartment.

I hit the doorbell with his name. It buzzes and the door clicks, unlocking. I slip inside to a small, cramped hallway with a staircase and an elevator. I wait by the elevator, which hums as it lowers and the form of a man comes into view.

Shoes first: dark loafers. Followed by loose, dark slacks and an olive-colored wool sweater. Finally, his face appears —that mane of dark, wavy hair, those sharp blue eyes peering out from underneath intense, furrowed eyebrows. That ever-present, annoyed frown.

The old elevator comes to a rickety halt. Dorian pulls open the gate.

"Boss," he says.

I slide my eyes over him. "Pet."

I step inside. It's a manual operation and he yanks the gate shut and cranks the elevator. It groans like it's annoyed to be put to use and shudders back to life before rising.

We stand side by side. He's a head and a half taller than me, even with the lift my boots give me. As we stand in silence, I can *feel* him. Being in Dorian's presence is a bit like being in the room with a live grenade. The tense, wound-tight energy of him.

A smarter woman would deactivate him. But I've always been more of a let's-pull-the-pin-and-see-what-happens-next kind of girl. I can't ignore the tingle of excitement that starts in my chest and spreads through the rest of my body.

"You're late," he says.

I scoff. "By two minutes."

"Try ten."

"Was it very hard for you?" I ask with mock concern. The muscle in his jaw flexes, because we both know the answer.

The elevator comes to a harrowing halt. He pulls back the gate, and I step directly into his apartment. I found this particular quirk of his apartment building jarring the first time I experienced it—how do you keep strangers from walking right into your apartment by accident? Dorian explained to me that the elevator has to be manually "called" to each specific floor. Whoever uses the elevator last is in charge of sending it to the next floor when someone rings it —a loud, nagging buzz. More irritating than luxurious, but it's from an era of Manhattan when buildings like these had twenty-four-seven doormen. Now, they're lucky if they get their trash picked up on time.

In case it's not clear: I know more about Dorian's elevator than I know about Dorian. More on that later.

He's got a great space—a wide, yawning living room, flanked by an open kitchen and bar. The apartment is a wash of deep, earthy red and brown tones. It's clean, but cluttered, namely with books which overflow from his bookshelf, stack up against the wall, and cover nearly every inch of his apartment. He has a gorgeous half-moon window, but the curtains are almost always drawn, cursing the place to dim lamp lighting.

I step inside and shrug out of my coat, scarf, and beanie. Dorian takes them and folds them over a chair at his bar.

"Shoes," I say. He kneels and begins undoing my laces, helping me out of my boots.

I tease my fingers through his hair. Soft hair. In the past, my type was typically rough, dirty boys. Boys covered in stains who needed to be hosed down before you jumped into bed with them. My Dorian is a vain, well-groomed boy, and his hair products are probably more expensive than mine. He always smells nice, fresh. And that is Dorian in a nutshell—he gives the *appearance* of being put together so no one notices he'd really just pieces of a man duct-taped together with a caustic sense of humor and a generous heap of self-loathing.

A broken boy, maybe. But for the next thirty minutes, he's *my* broken boy.

"I just had the weirdest fucking conversation," I tell him.

"Tell me about it," he says.

The funny thing is—he actually means it. Our play sessions have started doubling as my own personal therapy sessions. He doesn't care what I talk about, so long as I keep teasing him. In fact, the more disinterested I am in pleasing him, the harder he gets. So. *Win-win.*

I use his head for balance as I step out of one boot, then the other. "I was grabbing a drink across the street, and this guy started hitting on me."

Dorian stands. I put my fingers to his chest and nudge him backwards. I guide him into his adjoining living room and he follows my lead, sitting down on the couch.

"Was he attractive?" he asks.

I plop down beside him, cuddling up like we're on a sleepover. I tickle my fingers down his chest.

"Very. Rugged. Rough. I wanted to suck the tattoos

straight off his body." I pinch his sweater between my fingers. "Take this off."

He makes a small *hm* noise. I can see him struggling with it—stuck somewhere between jealousy and desire. Dorian has an abundance of *I shouldn't want this* kinks, which makes him especially fun to torment.

He pulls the sweater and the t-shirt underneath over his head and tosses them on the floor. He has a gorgeous figure, a trim chest with a light dusting of dark hair that runs a trail down the center of his body.

"What happened next?" he asks.

I touch his chest, savoring the heat of his skin. I trace my fingers absently over his body, feeling the hardness of muscles, the sweet twitches at his abdomen when I graze the line of his belt. "He discovered I'm thirty-five. And he said *good for you.*"

His eyes fix on me. "He complimented you? That asshole."

"I'm serious. It made me feel…I don't know. *Old.*"

"You don't look a day over sixty-five, boss."

I grab him by the chin. "Someone's really asking for a beating today, aren't they?"

Those blue eyes meet mine. "No idea what you mean." Dorian's voice is deep and smooth. Too smooth. It's time to rattle him. I pinch his nipple, giving a little tug. His breath catches, which sends a lovely rush of heat through me. I do the same to the other nipple.

"My point is," I continue, "thirty-five *is* young. There shouldn't *be* any good for you. There should just be…*good.* I mean, did I miss a memo? Is thirty-five is the end of the line?" I drop his nipples and move my nails up and down his body. I dig them in so they leave lovely, red lines across his pale skin. His fingers tighten around the couch cushions, but he knows better than to move. "I mean, it's like everyone expects me to have my shit together. Like I should be married with children and sensible life at this point. But I feel like I'm just finding myself, you know?"

"I know." His eyes are half closed, and as much as he's trying to be still, trying to be a good boy, he can't help himself and he arches into my hand, hips lifting, hunting for friction. With every pass of my nails, he's dropping further and further into subspace, the brattiness leaving his body like an exorcism.

"What do you think? Are we old?"

He tilts his head, looking me in the eyes. "I think we're just getting started."

I can't help but grin at that. "Take off your pants."

"Yes, boss."

He does. He unbuttons, pulls his zipper down, and pushes his pants down his legs. He's wearing navy blue boxer-briefs that barely contain the man inside—the fabric gripping his strong thighs. Dorian is unfairly well-endowed and his cock swells obscenely against the stretch of his shorts. There's a small, dark wet patch at the tip of him.

I won't lie—it's a thrill, seeing evidence of the effect I have on him. I cup the space under his chin, gripping him by the jaw like a bad dog. The scuff of his trimmed beard is delightfully rough in my palm. "What is this?" I chastise. "A mess? Your cock is weeping already. Pathetic."

He pants against my hand, his breath short and rapid. "You told me to edge myself until you got here."

"Mm. I guess I did say that, huh?"

I drag my nails slowly down the center of his body. I follow the dusting of dark hair from his navel. I'm careful to avoid his stiff, leaking cock, even as his hips rise towards my touch.

He loves this. And I love that he loves this. It makes the

blood in my veins sing with a power I've never known before.

"How long has it been?"

His face reddens.

"Don't get shy now. I know you're counting the days."

"A week."

"Has it been that long since I let you come? Poor baby. You must be really fucking desperate. What do you think... have you been a good boy or bad?"

"Bad." We love a self-aware king.

"Should we make it a month?"

A groan leaves his throat. I slide my hands up his thighs. I lean against him and draw my lips over his throat. I suck the skin there, put my teeth around it, and give him a small bite.

"Harder," he begs.

"It's going to leave a mark," I warn.

"I know. I want you to."

Delicious. I pull my lips against his skin, sinking my teeth in this time. I hear his breath hitch at the pain and his thighs tense under my hands. I suck, tasting the heat of his neck, and when I pull back, the skin is already bright red.

His breath is coming in short gasps. I nuzzle against his ear. "I bet you'd love it if I touched you right now, wouldn't you?"

He swallows. His Adam's apple bobs. "Yes."

"Should I give you...thirty-five strokes? One worship stroke for each year I've blessed the earth with my presence?"

He whimpers. I grin. I tease a hand up his cock. I palm him through the fabric. "Are you glad I'm not twenty-one now, you degenerate?"

"Yes, boss."

"Do you wish I was forty? Fifty? Eighty?" He groans. I nip his ear. "Will you fuck me when I'm a GILF, puppy?"

"I'd fuck you until your knuckles went white gripping your walker, boss."

I let out a breath of a laugh. I nibble his jaw. "You'd be so lucky. Pull these down." I snap a finger against the rim of his briefs. He pushes them off his hips, leaving them bunched around his ankles. His cock stands stiff and eager at attention.

"So eager for me. Horny bastard." I trace my fingertip slowly—so slowly—from the base of him to the tip.

His face is beat red, the veins in his neck rising to the surface. He's in delicious agony, and he fucking loves it.

And my deep, dark secret?

I love it, too.

I rest my head on his chest. I can hear his heart ricocheting wildly. I take my time with him, slowly grazing my fingertip up and down the length of him. The velvet hard skin. He's slick with his own pre-cum, and it makes it easy for me to tease him like this. When I reach the head of him, I swirl my finger around the red, slick tip. He chokes.

His eyes shut tightly, eyebrows twisted. His legs begin to tremble.

I bite my lip. "My sweet, shaky boy. Is this too much stimulation? Too much and not enough all at once?"

I pull his earlobe between my lips and suck lightly. He loves dirty talk, so I sigh here contently. "I'll tell you what. If you're very, very good and if you can take these thirty-five strokes without coming…I'll give you a reward. I'll put my lips on you. You'd like that, wouldn't you?" I wrap my fingers around him, gripping. He groans. I start to stroke—slow, long pulls. "God. I bet that would feel like heaven to your poor, abandoned cock. How many sucks do you think it would take? Two? Three? Before you popped off? You wouldn't last a second. Oh, shit. I was supposed to be counting, wasn't it? Hmm...should we just start over? One...two..."

But time I get to *twenty*, he's trembling. I'm testing his limits. I know this because he always holds off begging as long as he can, but now the word finally falls from his lips: "Please..."

I let out a content hum. "What's that? *Please*? Please what?" I stroke him with one hand and move the other hand to his mouth. He opens for me and I press my fingers passed his lips. I hook my hand on his jaw. "Please tighter? Faster?"

I tighten my grip and start to pull him in rapid, slick strokes. He groans, protesting, but his pleas for me to slow down come garbled with my fingers in his mouth, and I pretend I can't hear him. "Just like that?" I ask. "Is that what you're saying? More on the head?" He's leaking badly now, the achy muscle throbbing in my grip. His breath shakes, eyebrows furrowed, trying *so hard* to be a good boy. If things get too intense, he has safe words he can use—the trigger phrase *red* to get me to stop at any moment. But he won't. He begs, complains, whines, because he loves it.

He loves the way I ruin him.

"Thirty-two," I count my strokes. "Thirty-three...wouldn't it be so sad if I stopped right now? Dorian and his *blue, blue Christmas...*"

"*Fuck!*" The threat pushes him over the edge. He shoots and I immediately pull my hand away. White, sticky splashes of Dorian hit my dress, his stomach, his thigh. His cock flexes angrily and his hips rut forward, but there's nothing but empty air. He has more to give. He wants more. But without any friction, he can't properly finish himself, and he hangs on that agonizing edge.

I drop my hand from his mouth, move it to his throat instead. I grip and his pulse jumps against my fingers as he struggles through the ruined orgasm. "Mmm," I hum. "I wonder what's worse. Not coming for a whole week...or coming just enough to get a taste of what you're missing?"

His eyes roll into the back of his head. "Fuck," he swears again, this time under his breath.

I grin. "You made a mess on my dress, bad boy. What are you going to do about it?"

"Clean it up, boss."

I don't have to tell him what to do. He knows. He gets up, briefs still tangled around his thighs, and falls to his knees in front of me. His strong hands grip my legs. He drops his head in my lap. I feel the wet heat of his tongue through the fabric of my dress as he licks his spilled seed from me.

I weave my fingers through his hair. "That's it...there's my good boy..."

He moans. He nuzzles between my legs. His nose dives underneath my dress and his dark, trim beard prickles against my inner thigh. I hear him inhale deeply. He wants to taste me, but can't—won't—without my permission.

The thought is tempting. Teasing him has gotten me worked up, and the damp fabric of my panties kisses my swollen cunt. I pull his hair, lightly tugging the roots. Encouraging him closer, until he's smothered against my panties. I feel the hard bridge of his nose nuzzling my clit, and we slide together. I grind my clothed pussy against his face, the energy between us sloppy and frantic.

"Dorian?"

"Yes?" His voice is tight with desperation.

I rake my nails down the nape of his neck. "It's time for me to go."

He groans. "But you just got here."

"How much more time do you need? Thirty minutes? More like thirty seconds, am I right?" I nudge my leg between his and feel his cock against my ankle. He's still swollen and hard and when I rub my foot against him, I'm rewarded with a shudder. "Too bad. I've got a plans."

His head tilts up so he can look me in the eyes. "With a man?"

Not gonna lie, the sharp jealousy in his voice makes me clench with pleasure.

I cock my head. "That's not very bi-friendly of you. I might have a girlfriend. Ever thought of that? Maybe if we get tired of having multiple, earth-shattering orgasms, I'll pop by tonight just so I can show off this pathetic, desperate puppy-man I keep around for laughs."

"Don't," he says, but the want in his voice betrays him.

I grin. "Pull yourself together."

I press a chaste kiss to the top of his head. It's a simple, but clear signal. *Our session is over.*

I push him away and he sits back on his heels. I rise to my feet, stepping around him, and readjust. I fix my dress back over my hips. Heat thrums through my veins, my heartbeat pounding, slowly returning to normal.

"Dove." I glance up. Dove—not boss. Small delineations to acknowledge that we've both exited the scene. Dorian stands in front of me, his pants slung loosely over his hips.

Even I have to admit, he's kind of hot like this. If you're into grumpy tall men with tight, trim bodies and a V-line that outlines his hips. He tugs his fingers through his messy hair, attempting to pull himself together. Some people pull off the *just fucked* look. He does one better; he has a *completely fucked up* look—charmingly disheveled, short of breath, eyes that wander around with a confused *where am I? what year is it? what's my name?* expression.

He is so cute when he's sex-stupid.

He pulls himself together enough to close the distance between us and holds up a small box wrapped in red and black paper. "Merry Christmas."

I take it gingerly, like it might grow teeth and snap at me at any moment. "You got me a present?"

He retracts his hands, shoving them back in his pockets. "Don't get too excited. It's just a little something."

The gift is meticulously wrapped, the edges perfectly flattened against the thin rectangle, the ribbon in a perfect knot. I slid off the ribbon, gracelessly tear off the paper, and pop open the box.

There's a beanie sitting inside. It might seem silly to everyone else, but beanies are *my thing*. I've always got one on. So, truthfully, it's actually a kind of thoughtful gift.

I'm touched, despite myself.

I turn the hat over. It's a grey beanie with a pigeon patch stitched on the front of it.

He explains: "I was going to get you a hat with a dove on it, but they were all carrying olive branches and I thought, *peace and harmony* doesn't really suit you."

"So you thought, *rat with wings? Street vermin?*"

A smile twitches at the corner of his mouth. "If the beak fits."

Dorian is a brat. And if we were still in the scene, his big mouth would be getting him into a world of trouble right now.

But, since we're no longer in the scene, I allow myself to grin at his cheekiness.

"I love it. Thank you."

"Don't mention it." His eyes flicker over me. He frowns. He touches my hip and rubs his thumb over the dark stain he left. "Leave your dress. I'll have it cleaned."

"Alright." In one, swift move, I yank my dress over my head and drop it to the floor. He blinks. His eyes drift over my body, now only in panties, a bra, and a beanie. The muscle in his jaw flexes as he admires the body he'll never touch. Never fuck.

That's the arrangement we have. Still, I enjoy basking in it every now and then.

A woman shouldn't have this much power. It's liable to give her all sorts of mean, no-good ideas.

I take my coat off the back of his chair and pull it over my shoulders. I tie it off at my waist. "Call me a cab."

His gaze darkens. "Absolutely not."

I tilt my head. "Excuse me?"

"You're not leaving the house like that." His voice is tight, possessive. He grips his own wrist, as though he has to physically restrain himself, shaking out the thought of me walking around New York with only a bra and panties under my coat. "Hold on."

He vanishes into his bedroom. He returns seconds later with a shirt and pair of pants folded up in his hands.

"Thanks." I pull them both on. They smell like him. They swallow me. "You're a real gentleman."

"A gentleman that comes all over your clothes," he counters.

"Mm. My favorite kind." I lean my entire body against his. Toe-to-toe, I'm so short next to him, the top of my head hitting his clavicle. He's so hard—and I don't just mean the bulge against my hip. I mean everywhere—hard chest, flat stomach. A gargoyle chiseled out of goddamn stone. I inhale him; he smells like soap and the musk of desire.

I tilt my head upwards, chin on his chest, and he tilts down to meet me. We don't kiss—but I rock my hips against his—a slow roll—and he's a very good boy, he doesn't grip me or grind against me the way I know he wants to. Instead, his eyes close, his shuddery breath warms my lips, and he goes very still, letting me tease him, savoring it. Because he knows the second I leave, I'm gone, and he'll be left with nothing but ache in my absence.

"Merry Christmas, pet," I tell him.

I extract my body from his. He takes me down the elevator and escorts me out. The second his door clicks locked behind me, my phone buzzes. He's texted:

DORIAN

Miss you already, boss.

I smile. Merry Christmas to me, indeed.

2

GIRLS ONLY ON THE FIRE ESCAPE

Dove. Now.

"Okay," Ophelia gestures with a bottle of rose, waving it over the fire escape, "million-dollar idea. A hamster wheel, but for humans."

"A treadmill," I say. "I think you're thinking about a treadmill."

She sighs. "But where the *fun* in that?"

We sit across from each other on the fire escape, legs tangled. We pass the bottle back and forth as the city honks and clatters below us.

Ophelia is my roommate, my confidant, and my best friend. When I die an untimely death, probably, in a freak garbage compactor accident, she'll be the one to clear my search history, destroy my eReader, and write an obituary that'll make my mother proud. She's an absolutely stunning woman, with long curly hair, and wide, intelligent eyes. Ophelia is an actress—currently only booking commercials and the odd off-off Broadway part, but she's working her way to a Tony, I'm sure of it. This is all fodder for her acceptance speech. She's constantly dressed like she's ready for the red carpet, too. While I rock my messy, thrift-store finds, Ophelia wears clothes like she's doing them a favor—currently wrapped up in a giant, faux-fur coat that makes her look like the bear at the end of *Midsommar*.

It's insanely cold out here, a biting forty degrees in a blanket of night, but our fire escape hangouts are *sacred*, so we brave the winter. There's a dusting of snow on the grated stairway and it's wet against my ass, but I ignore it.

Ophelia refills both our glasses. We should've stopped a bottle ago, but now we're well passed hangover territory and there's nothing to do but keep pushing forward.

"So you're coming to my birthday party tomorrow, yeah?" Ophelia says. Her dark eyes flash at me. It's a demand—not a request.

"Oh, shit. Is that tomorrow?"

"*Oh, shit*, my ass. You don't get to flake. Not on my birthday, bitch. Besides, I need witnesses."

"What, are you gonna kill Brody?"

"No," she says casually, "I'm going to marry him."

Bubbles go up my nose. I make a sound like I'm dying and gasp out, "What?"

"I think he's going to propose."

"That's..." I measure my words. "Is that good news or bad news?"

She shakes her head. "I know you're thinking he's going to break my heart," she says, the goddamn mind reader, "and yeah, maybe you're right. But I've gotta try, don't I?"

I twist up my mouth. "Do you? Do you *really*?"

"Fuck off with that *child-of-divorced-parents* shit."

I snort a laugh. One of those laughs laced with years of childhood pain—if you can't laugh about it, you'll cry, right? "Okay, but let me just make my point." I lift a finger.

"A year ago, you watched me get absolutely crushed by Shawn."

"Mount Shawn of Shit," Ophelia hisses. His name is still a curse in our apartment.

"Exactly. And it wrecked me. I can say that now. I put my heart out there and it ripped me apart. And now look at me. I'm not chasing love. No, I am grounded, and real, and doing things that make me happy. I spend all day eating cheese. I get all the tattoos I want and drink all the wine I want. And the only man in my life is a submissive who does whatever I want."

Her gaze measures me. "How *is* that going?"

"Great. I spend my Fridays making a grown man whimper and he does my dry cleaning."

Ophelia sucks in her teeth. "You're living the dream."

"Yes. Yes, I am."

I lay my head back. The fire escape is freezing, but I don't mind it. It's a cold relief, like those cucumbers they put on the backs of your eyes at a spa.

You can't see the stars in Brooklyn; the New York City lights are too blinding. But I can see streaks of black, an empty canvas where stars *should* be.

Ophelia's boot knocks against my leg. "Don't you miss it, though?"

"Miss what?"

"The Seekers Club. Playing. Submitting." She presses her lips together. "The Club misses *you*."

I feel like I've swallowed a bird, and it's trying to get out now, flapping its wings frantically, sending scratchy feathers scattering all around my chest.

I don't want to tell her the truth, but I can't lie to Ophelia, so I ask instead: "Do we have any pickles?"

3

THE SEEKERS CLUB

DOVE. Then.

I got into the kink lifestyle the way most people get into trouble—by reading too much.

Two years ago, I found myself in a large bookstore on 14th street. I'd moved to New York to attend an artist residency—which had been great news for my mom, not because she was sculpture and I was following in her visual art footsteps, but because I was finally out of the house and she had her studio to herself. Now that my residency was over, I was determined to plant myself in the city and stay out of mom's way. I found myself exploring every crack in the sidewalk, any strange, fringe community I could fit myself into. And New York City was full of them. Poets, performers, people who dressed up in dinosaur costumes and engaged in wrestling competitions every Saturday now. My investment in the *fringe and freak* was how I found myself sitting in a stiff folding chair and clutching my copy of *Damaged Hearts* by Quinn Siobhan. The crowd was packed—mostly women in yoga pants and ponytails—all wearing coy, shy smiles, all similarly clinging to their book.

The book in question was an (allegedly) semi-autobiographical, steamy romance about a married woman and her illicit affair. The story goes like this: Quinn is twenty-eight and in a rut. She just had her first child and she's exhausted. Her sex life with her husband, Mark, has completely dried up. Desperate, she decides to lean on familial ties. She enlists the help of Mark's playboy younger brother. She knows from her husband that his brother is into "strange and dark" things and participates in a kink club. So Quinn decides that, to spice things up in the bedroom, she's going to get him to teach her his devious tricks.

Poe (that's his scene name—*Poe*, after Edgar Allen) is a Dominant in the kink community. He reluctantly agrees and, for three hundred and fifty pages, he teaches her how to be a submissive. He spanks her. Chokes her. Puts her on her knees and degrades her. Teaches her safe words. Teaches her aftercare. And she takes her lessons to her marriage bed. Her marriage is finally growing heat again. But…and I think you can see where this is going…there's a second fire growing between Quinn and Poe.

Quinn—the real-life Quinn—was a gorgeous woman in her early forties. She had long, shiny black hair, dark eyes, and a svelte figure. A square-faced man with a salt-and-pepper beard sat in the chair behind her, his eyes frequently darting around the crowd. He seemed like a bodyguard, but by the way he constantly twisted his wedding ring, my guess was that this was the real-life Mark, her husband.

Quinn took the podium with confidence. She pushed her hair back, cracked open her book, and began to read:

The club was a cacophony of sights and sounds.

A woman was bound to an X-shaped structure. A man crawled on all fours with a muzzle. Another woman screamed as a whip lashed across her back.

I shivered and took a step back. Poe's strong body brushed against mine. His hand clasped over my arm.

"This way," he murmured into my ear. He led me through the chaos of the room. We found a quiet corner with a bench. He instructed me to straddle the bench, then he mirrored my position, taking a seat in front of me.

He set his bag down beside us. It was a leather satchel, the type of bag a professor might carry, but Poe's bag didn't hold textbooks. I watched as he unzippered it, rummaged through, and pulled out a small, leather paddle.

"What if I can't take it?" I blurted out. "The pain."

His icy blue eyes met mine. "I'll never give you more than you can take," he told me. "If you want to stop at any time, you use your safe word. Tell me your safe word."

"Red."

"Good." A rare smile from him. I'd passed the test. "Hands behind you. Grip the bench."

I obeyed, clutching the seat behind me. The position forced my back to arch, giving him access to my body. His large hand pushed my short skirt up, baring my thigh.

"Keep your eyes on mine," he said.

I forced myself to stare into his gaze. Those intense, blue eyes never left mine. Slowly, he inched the paddle up my leg, drawing a line from my knee to my hip.

"Kink is less about pain," he informed me. "It's about connection."

Suddenly, he flicked his wrist. The leather paddle whacked against my thigh, stinging the skin. I drew in a sharp gasp and instinctively turned my gaze to the paddle.

Quick as a snake, Poe grabbed my throat. His hand didn't

choke me, but it held me in a vice, forcing my chin up and my eyes back on his.

"What did I say?" His voice was a dark demand.

I could feel my pulse jumping against his fingers. Just like that, the rest of the club faded away. Everything in me was focused on those eyes, and that strong grip. I felt held. Safe. And aroused beyond belief. Outside—he was my brother-in-law. Here...we were something else entirely.

"Eyes on yours," I said.

"Good girl. Do you want me to keep going?"

I widened the spread of my legs, inviting him to the expanse of my thigh. "Please, sir."

He couldn't hide it—the effect that word had on him. His eyes widened, just slightly. His nostrils flared, pupils dilating, as he sucked in a deeper breath, trying to hide it. Slowly, he pet his thumb against the curve of my throat. I felt my nipples tighten into pebbles.

He snapped the paddle against my thigh again. It stung, but this time, I knew what to expect. The pain bloomed and then faded just as quickly, leaving a lovely, warm sensation in its wake. This time, my eyes never left his.

"You're a quick learner," he said. The heat in his voice sent a shiver down my spine. "Now let's see what else you can take."

Quinn finished her excerpt, and the audience clapped. My heart pounded in time with the applause. Poe and his obsessive, dirty domination had an uncanny hold on me.

There was time for questions from the audience. Q: Does she ever go all the way with Poe? (A: You'll have to read the next book to find out). Q: How does your husband feel about the book? (A: He has the patience of a saint). Q: Where is Poe now? (A: We don't talk much anymore).

My hand shot up. When I asked my question, my voice shook. "Is the club…um. Based on a real place?"

A knowing smile crossed Quinn's face. "Yes, but I'm sworn to secrecy."

Laughter from the group. I could feel my blush rising hot up my neck and through my cheeks. I was so embarrassed, I couldn't even bring myself to get my book signed. I just made a mad dash out the bookstore once the signing was over.

A voice stopped me with a: "Hey." I turned and found myself face-to-face with a city witch. Well, at least, that's what she looked like to me at the time. Her arms were covered in tattoos, she wore a bomber jacket and Doc Martens, and her hair was an explosions of tight curls around her face. Her copy of *Damaged Hearts* was as bent up and busted as mine. She looked as though she were torn straight from the pages of a Dashiell Hammett novel when she pushed off the wall and said, "Don't listen to that gatekeeping bitch. Are you looking for a kink club?"

A blush creeped up my neck. "I mean…I don't know…I guess I was just curious if it exists…for science…"

"Oh, it exists." She reached into her large side bag and rummaged around until she pulled out a pen. She grabbed my wrist and scribbled her number up my forearm. "I'm Ruby. But my real friends call me Ophelia."

"Sadie."

"Text me and I'll get you the address."

I texted her. Right in the subway. I couldn't even wait to get home. She sent back:

Friday at 7 pm. Meet me at the bodega on 132nd Street.

Then she sent me a link to an app.

* * *

The app was called: The Seekers' Club.

The icon was the image of two keys crisscrossed together. When I opened it, it asked me to set up a profile.

I punched in my name, my pronouns, and then it asked:

What are you Seeking?

What *was* I seeking for? It gave options. Was I looking for a Dominant? A submissive? A sadist? A mentor? A friend?

One of the options gave me a strange, unexpected knot in my throat.

Community, it said.

I hadn't felt part of a community in…ever, maybe. My parents divorced when I was six. They split the twins; dad took my brother across the country to California while I stayed with my mom in Massachusetts, where she had her sculpting studio and taught art classes to during the week. My brother became a stranger with my eyes. My father hated me because I'd "chosen the wrong parent," even though I'd been too young to realize I was making a choice when I reached up in the court room and took my mother's outreached hand.

These little, split-second decisions we make. They haunt us.

I picked *Community* and kept going. The app wanted a profile image. I uploaded a selfie from the nose down, so I wouldn't be easily recognized.

Profile complete, I was now able to scroll through *other* people's profiles. I was floored to see how many different kinky people existed in New York City alone. All types, too— one called himself a "floor mat." Another was a "puppy seeking a master." And, of course, profile after profile of 20-something hot Doms, seeking a "good girl."

My mouth went dry. It felt like I'd struck gold.

You could "match" with certain people by hitting the "match" button under their profile. I didn't dare. I let myself be a voyeur, just watching from the sidelines for now.

When Friday rolled around, I got dressed and met at the location Ophelia had mentioned—a spot in Harlem, a couple blocks from where the subway let out. I checked my phone repeatedly. I felt like a lunatic, waiting for a stranger in front of a bodega.

A fall chill was crisp in the air and I was shivering in a tight dress and kitten heels. The bodega's "open" sign flickered behind me and a couple of guys hung around the ice box, drinking and chatting with each other.

I checked the time on my phone. It was a little past seven. I could leave. Pretend I never came here. I could—

I heard a shriek, and then the shout: "You made it!" I glanced up to see Ophelia bounding towards me. She closed the distance between us quickly and squeezed me tight like we were old friends. She was wearing a loose sweater and a short skirt, and when she hugged me, I got a heavy whiff of her flowery perfume.

She pulled back and gripped my arms. "Ready? You look ready."

I couldn't help but grin. "So ready."

She laced her fingers in mine and took me down the street. We walked down the block and came to a stop in front of a nondescript brownstone apartment. Ophelia climbed the steps and pulled out her phone, motioning for me to do the same.

"Check your app," she told me.

I pulled up the Seekers' Club app. She directed me to press the key button on the bottom righthand corner.

Four numbers popped up. 4-9-8-8.

There was a keypad on the door, and she punched the numbers in. "It changes every week," she told me. "Security, or whatever. Hey—what should I call you? A lot of us have scene names. So, for example—" she put her hand on her chest. "I'm Ruby, but inside, they know me as Ophelia. Because I'm—I don't know—tragic and dramatic, I guess."

My brain raced as I tried to quickly come up with a scene name. A pigeon fluttered by us, pecking at something at the ground. Pigeon? No, that wasn't sexy, what about...?

"Dove," I said.

Ruby/Ophelia grinned. "Dove it is."

A light on the keypad turned green and the door clicked open, granting us access. Inside, we stepped through a short foyer, passing underneath a hanging lantern, where the apartment opened up to a living space. It was decorated in dark, rich wood and velvet furniture. Soft, thumping music came from a hidden sound system. The low lighting gave the space a cozy, hypnotizing vibe.

There were a couple people hanging out already. They looked up at us curiously when we entered. A blonde popped up from a leather seat and came over to us. She wore pigtails in her hair and an array of pins on her sleeve—one that said "she/her," a pin of the trans pride flag, and an adorable pin of a rat with a slice of pizza in its mouth.

Ophelia introduced us. "Dove, meet Princess. She's the baby of the group, but she's also the house mom, so her word is law. Disobey, and you're out on your ass."

"You're new here," Princess said. "Welcome. If you don't mind signing in..."

Signing in included handing over my license and filling out a couple forms—a non-disclosure and a liability waiver. I felt a bit like I was about to enter a kinky rollercoaster. Princess offered to give me a tour, but Ophelia took it upon herself to show me around. She'd adopted me, and I was grateful for the hand-holding. Literally. She didn't let go of my hand as she guided me through.

"There are three floors," she informed me. "They get kinkier as you go up, basically. The first floor is the lounge—

we've got a bar, snacks. You can hang out here, mingle. A lot of people come down here for after care. Second floor is for public play—that's where you've got your St. Andrews' crosses, paddle benches, that sort of thing. Top floor is invite-only—that's where you've got your private rooms. Basically, you can go up there to fuck. Any questions?"

So, so many. My head was spinning with them. "It looks like someone's house."

Ophelia shrugged. "It is. He comes around now and then. We just bless Daddy Warbucks for letting us turn this place into a den of sin every Friday." She flopped in a chair near the unlit fireplace and looked at me. Her eyes slid over me, examining. "So, what's your type?"

A heat climbed my neck. "What do you mean?"

"Are you a submissive? Dominant? Sadist? Rope bunny?"

She might as well have been speaking in Klingon.

"I'm...not sure."

"Let me put it this way—are you a Poe or a Quinn?"

I bit my lip. "A Quinn."

Ophelia winked. "I got you. Stay here." She hopped up from her seat and crossed the room to the group of guys in the corner. They were about our age, maybe younger—late twenties, early thirties. Stacked. Gorgeous. I felt myself melting into the vintage wallpaper—the awkward new girl. I watched as Ophelia slipped her arms around a guy's strong middle. She whispered into his ear and a grin slid across his mouth. They had an easy intimacy with each other. Seconds later, she took him by the hand and guided him over to us.

I took stock of him as he approached—hair cut so short, it was almost buzzed. Brown skin. Vibrant, green eyes that made my stomach flip.

Ophelia ran her hand up his arm, presenting him to me. "This is Carver. Carver, Dove. This is her first time."

"Welcome to the Club," he said. His voice had a darkness to it that made me shiver.

"Thanks."

Ophelia cocked her head. "Do you want to play?"

I blinked. "With him? Isn't he your…um…?"

"My…?"

"Boyfriend?"

They exchanged a glance, then broke into laughter.

"Fuck no." Ophelia shook her head. "I know the book made it seem all like—ooh, sexy, scandalous. And yeah, sure. Kink is hot. But you'll have way more fun if you just think of this as a place where a group of friends hang out and sometimes spank each other."

Just like that, something switched in me.

I had permission. Permission to *have fun*.

I extended my hand the way a princess might—wrist limp—towards the Dominant. "Okay," I said. "Let's play. Please. Sir."

He grinned, took my hand, and said, "Let's have some fun, little Dove."

* * *

Carver took me to the second floor. We talked for almost an hour—what was I comfortable with? What was I not comfortable with? Then I got spanked until my ass was black and blue.

Ophelia and I played all night. We took turns—she would "spot me," as she called it, which meant she'd watch as the Dominant and I played, just so she could check in with me every now and then and make sure the scene was running smoothly. Then I would spot her, watching as she got spanked, or whipped, or tied up. Around midnight, we ditched the dom in favor of pastrami sandwiches from the all-night bodega. We ate sloppy sandwiches out of greasy bags and laughed until we choked. I felt high or drunk, even though I was neither of those things. It was one of those nights when you could feel the magic of the city rattling around like subway cars under your feet.

"I feel so fucking good right now," I told her.

"Sub euphoria, baby," she purred. A rat scurried around the black trash bags piled up on the street. Ophelia plucked a corner of bread from her sandwich and tossed it at the creature, who sat on his hunches, took it in his little paws, and started munching.

"I always wanted a sister," I blurted out, feeling stupidly sentimental.

A grin stretched across Ophelia's mouth. "I *have* sisters," she said. "Too many of them. They steal your clothes and beat you up for touching their food." She slung her arm around my shoulders. When she pulled me close, I got a strong whiff of her floral perfume. "*This,*" she said. "Is so much better. Welcome home, baby."

Home. That's what it felt like. The club. Ophelia. This pastrami sandwich. The rat on the corner. It all felt like *home.*

4

BIG DUMB DOGS

Dove. Then.

I went back the next Friday. And the next. And every Friday after that.

I was hooked.

I woke up with bruises on my skin that made me feel deliciously alive. I spent my weekdays painting like a mad woman. I'd started a series of paintings based on my nights at the club—a painting of a woman with rope for hair that knotted and tangled all around her. A painting of a man with the head of a dog and paws for hands. A painting of a couple whose limbs were fused together, whose lips melted when they kissed. I'd even gotten bold enough to enter a few into competitions and my boldness was rewarded with a couple local showings.

Every week, I counted the days until Friday.

Ophelia taught me everything I needed to know. Lessons like...

Rule #1: Doms are like really dumb dogs, for the most

part. Give them what they want and you'll have them wrapped around your finger. They think they're in control, but they're not, because...

Rule #2: As the submissive, you control the scene. Always. You say when it stops. You say how far it goes. Safe words are your friend.

Rule #3: It's not about sex, but sometimes, it's *fucking hot*. And most Doms (remember: big, dumb dogs) still won't know how to find your clit. If you want to come, find the oldest looking leather mommy. She'll make your legs shake. I'm talking *multiple* orgasms, baby.

Rule #4: And if you *want* to have sex, go to the top floor for that action. Don't let them take you home. The Club is a sanctuary, a safe space. Once you leave that safe space, guys think they can get away with anything. Don't let them. What happens at the Club, stays in the Club.

Rule #5: Have fun. Seriously. That's the most important part. The second a Dom hurts you because he's angry or humiliates you in a way that makes you feel *actually* bad about yourself—that's a huge red flag. Play should be fun. So *have fun*.

We went through doms like rented outfits. Try this one on for size, and then the other. I went through the alphabet of kinky dominants:

A is for Angel who took selfies after spankings.

B is for Bella who wanted me to bark like a dog.

C is for Chris who tied me up and then mansplained the plot of *Alien* to me.

D is for Devil who forgot to mention his wife at home.

I tried it all. Sadistic tops. Leather mommies. Pleasure doms. Except...the masochist in me was always drawn to the people that hurt me.

Really, *really* hurt me.

Which is how I met Shawn.

Shawn was a burly guy with curly red hair. I met him on the first floor—the "lounge"—where he was mingling with some of the other doms. I noticed his laugh first. It was a big, booming sound. I was attracted to his laugh, the strong way he carried his body, and the hair on his arms.

I said, "I'm Dove."

He said, "Shawn."

I said, "That's some creative scene name."

He said, "It's just my fucking name. I don't play games."

He said it with a smile, though. He was an asshole. Naturally, that meant I was in love.

* * *

I broke Rule #4. I let Shawn take me home the first night we played together.

Shawn fucked like a man. That hard, selfish rutting. His fingers squeezed my hips and made me feel claimed. When he came, he collapsed beside me, and didn't offer to finish me.

Instead, he motioned to his chest and said: "Come on. Be a good girl and cuddle."

Why was I attracted to this?

I wanted to drown in his musk. His sweat was like a pheromone to me. I could hardly wait to tell Ophelia, who'd become my kink-sister. When I found her at the club the next week, I cornered her in the longue and spilled my guts, barely taking a breath in between sentences. She listened, nodded, eyes widening in places, laughing in others. Then, suddenly, she took my hand and squeezed, stopping me.

"Hey," she said. "I'm *so* proud of you for taking what you want. Seriously. Go slut girl summer. But can we pick this up later? I *really* want to hear the end of it, but someone important just walked in."

Important? What was more important than my new man crush? But—

"Yeah," I said. "Of course."

I watched as Ophelia crossed the room. Ophelia—objectively the most stunning woman at the club—had her eyes on someone. I expected Tall, Dark, and Handsome. Idris Elba, maybe.

Instead, something weird happened.

A guy entered—average height, slim build. A face that was easily lost in a crowd. In his forties, maybe, with tight curls that were going grey. Not hot the way guys like Carver were hot—all brawn and youthful arrogance. He was just…some guy in jeans and dad shoes. Forgettable, except for a purple birthmark that curved from his cheek down his neck.

Ophelia didn't perform her normal peacocking: flirting and parading around the dom until they were practically dragging her upstairs. Instead, she immediately lowered herself to the floor in front of him. She put her hands on her knees, bowed her head, and dropped her eyes on the ground.

Doms were people we obeyed in public, but laughed about behind their backs. They were bossy little boys who were fun when you needed a spanking, but easy to discard after.

This wasn't that. This was Ophelia unlike I'd ever seen her before—truly, reverently, completely submissive.

I watched, hypnotized by the exchange.

The man crouched down, lowering himself to Ophelia's level. He put his hand on her shoulder. He tilted his head to her ear. I could see him whispering.

Without raising her eyes, she answered clearly: "Yes, Master."

He pulled a slim rope out of his pocket. He looped it around her wrists and then pulled it between her arms, latching them together. The rope left a small tail and he used it like a leash to guide her up. She followed him, her head still bowed, her wrists bound in front of her.

I felt Carver over my shoulder. I wasn't the only one watching them. "Who's that?" I asked him.

"Phantom," he answered. "He runs this place. He's Ophelia's Dom."

Her…Dom? The Ophelia I knew had *doms*. Plural. Casual guys she played around with.

But this felt different.

Carver nudged me with his shoulder. "C'mon. Let's grab a seat. It's usually a good show."

I followed Carver upstairs to the second floor.

Phantom and Ophelia had claimed the rigging room. There were a few chairs around the room, some already taken. Carver and I took the loveseat against the wall. Ophelia was face down on the carpet. Her dress had been removed and now, clad in her bra and panties, she was wrapped up in a cocoon of rope. Phantom was winding strands of purple rope around and around her. Her legs and arms were tied together behind her, so her body stretched backwards in an arch. I was used to bratty Ophelia—the Ophelia who would goad on her dominants and talk back to them. Now, she wasn't moving, wasn't speaking. I would've thought she'd fallen asleep, except every now and then Phantom would stop what he was doing to lean over and murmur in her ear, and she would nod and respond with a soft *Yes, Master* or *No, Master*.

It should've been boring, sitting there and just watching him tie her up. Instead, I found myself captivated by it. Each strand of rope seemed to pull Ophelia deeper and deeper into a trance. Then, when she was completely bound, he untied a rope that was cleated to the wall. As he gave it slack, a square device with four hooks lowered from the ceiling. I watched as he slotted the ropes from Ophelia around the hooks. Once she was secure, he returned to the cleat, strung it back through, and began to pull.

Ophelia lifted. It pulled her through the air until she was hanging like a human chandelier, arms and legs bound behind her.

My heart pounded in my chest. He lifted her until she was dangling in the air. Then he secured the rope and returned to her. I watched him check in with her again. She nodded. Gently, slowly, he began to slide his fingers over her skin. Down her stomach. Her legs. She shivered, squirmed, but she was completely immobile. When his gentle touches turned rougher with a smack on her thigh, she yelped helplessly.

He teased her with his hands. Then with a paddle. He could've had any part of her he wanted, but he stayed away from the space between her thighs. This wasn't sexual. This was something else—an exercise in trust.

Finally, he went to his box and pulled out a slender, long glass device. He spoke to her for a moment. Then he touched the device gently to her body. Every time it touched her body, Ophelia let out a sharp cry. Just the slightest touch made her shout out. I watched as he repeated it, and again, tapping the device against different spots of her body.

"Mercy!" Ophelia finally shouted. He immediately lowered the wand. He cradled her face in his other hand.

"I'm sorry," she sputtered. She was crying now. "I'm sorry."

Then, suddenly, she broke. She burst into tears. Big, heavy tears. I started to get up, wanting to comfort her, but Carver stopped me with a hand on my shoulder. He shook his head.

"Let her," he said. "She's okay. Watch."

Phantom undid a knot I couldn't see. Almost instantly, Ophelia was released from the suspension. She dropped into his arms and he held her, still cocooned in the rope.

He was saying something. Over and over. I couldn't hear it at first, not over her loud sobs. And then it hit me.

"Good girl." Again and again. He held her as she cried, cradling her tightly.

Carver's arm found its way across the back of the loveseat, over my shoulders. The energy in the audience had shifted—everyone was aroused, excited, itching to play. But as I watched Phantom give Ophelia aftercare, it felt as though someone had taken an ice cream scooper and used it to remove my heart from my chest.

Playing was fun. Getting spanked was fun.

But I wanted *more*.

I wanted what they had. The trust. That connection. The way their bodies seemed to know each other.

The ache was so bad, the backs of my eyes stung. I had to look away.

"Sorry," I told Carver. I got up and left, quickly rushing out of the room.

I left the Club. I felt like a woman on a mission. The subway took me away from Harlem, downtown, and into Brooklyn. I followed the line all the way to Shawn's apartment.

His apartment building had a short step and a long line of apartments with a fisheye doorbell camera. I rang his door-bell and waited.

"Yo," he said.

"Hey. It's me." When there wasn't any response, I added, "Dove."

"What's up?"

Could he see me? I wasn't sure. I chanced it anyway. I got on my knees on the dirty New York City curb. "I want to be yours," I announced.

The intercom crackled. "What? Sorry. Can't hear anything in this."

"I—" a man feeding pigeons across the street started to laugh. I ignored him. I yelled into the camera: "I want to be your submissive, sir!"

A pause. My knees were starting to hurt, and I tried not to let my brain wonder how much pigeon poop had collected here.

Finally, his voice came through again. "You like pizza?"

"Um…yes."

"Your first task: go get us a pie. Don't come back until you have it."

"What sort of…toppings?"

"Guess."

I couldn't help it. My heart fluttered. I grinned. "Yes, sir."

* * *

Being Shawn's submissive was not like Ophelia and Phantom.

But it wasn't bad, either.

I'd come over to his place. He'd play videogames and then he'd spank me. For aftercare, we'd eat pizza. On the weekends, he introduced me to low-lit, hipster bars in Bushwick where he seemed to know everybody. We played trivia night. He showed me off as his kinky, cute girlfriend. It was comfortable and cozy.

We clicked. He was my age—mid-thirties—with a burly body, a ginger beard, and a dark and twisted sense of humor that I found magnetic. He was one of those easy, casual dominants. The kind of guy who didn't take himself too seriously, but when he was on, he was *on*. I loved being his sweet, submissive partner. I wore pretty, floral dresses that he picked out. He preferred blondes, and I didn't have the money for a hair salon, so Ophelia and I grabbed box dye and nearly burned my scalp off turning my dark, auburn hair into a bright, platinum blonde. I had a soft, black collar that I kept around my neck as a sign of my devotion. I greeted him at the door on my knees. I asked permission to kiss him. I melted when he spanked my bottom or held my throat. I liked the way it felt to come home and just shut my brain off. I liked letting someone else make all the decisions.

Although we were a "vanilla" couple in public, on Fridays, we could be our true selves. We went to the club together and played. I wasn't allowed to play with anyone else—that was a limit of his—but I didn't want to. I liked being his and only his.

I told my mom about Shawn. "Does he love you?" she asked. Her voice was distracted, and I was on speaker phone. I could imagine her with her hands in clay, her hair pulled back into that tight ponytail to keep it clean.

"I'm not sure," I said, prodding the bear, "but he calls me a good girl when he spanks me, so I'll take it."

"That's nice, honey," she said, not having heard me at all, or maybe not caring, her attention a million miles away.

And it *was* nice to be Shawn's. It was perfect. For a while, anyway.

But after a couple of months, he started coming up with reasons not to go to the club. He'd set up drinks with friends. He'd make it a "surprise" date night. We started playing less and less at home.

And then, one Friday, I went to the Club alone and waited for him to meet me there. But all my texts went unanswered. I sat on the lower level, warming the bar stool for a full hour before the realization hit me: he wasn't coming.

I felt hot all over, uncomfortable. Embarrassed. When I got home, I found Shawn in the dark. The only light came from the TV. He had his headset on and he was playing a first-person shooter.

I flicked on the ceiling lights. He grunted in disapproval, like a vampire.

"Hey." I said. No response. He was too glued to the screen. I went into the living room and sat in the chair closest to the television. I unzipped my heels, dropping them to the floor and stretching my toes.

"I waited for you at the club," I continued. I didn't try to hide the irritation in my voice.

"Yeah. I'm not going anymore."

"Why not?" I stared at him, but his eyes never left the screen.

"It's kid stuff. A bunch of freaks playing kinky make believe. Grow up."

His words hit me like a shock of cold water. For a second, I couldn't speak. "But…they're my friends."

"Get new friends."

Heat climbed my neck. "You don't have to be a dick about it."

Suddenly, his eyes snapped towards me. "What'd you say?"

His voice had heat. A loud, angry baritone I wasn't familiar with. It stopped me in my tracks. Which is when it hit me:

We weren't in a scene. I had no safe word here.

"Nothing," I said. My voice was so quiet, I could barely hear it.

* * *

We stopped going to the club completely.

I was his vanilla girlfriend now. We went out with *his* friends. We did whatever *he* wanted to do. I wasn't his obedient submissive, and yet I'd never felt more controlled.

Ophelia kept calling, wondering why I'd fallen off the face

of the earth. I gave her excuse after excuse, until finally even her texts became less and less frequent.

Finally, in December, she sent me:

OPHELIA

Hey. I know it's been a while, but I'm having a birthday party this Friday. All Seekers. It'd mean a lot if you were there. Love you.

I was so guilty, I felt sick. Physically ill. Finally, I put my foot down with Shawn. I was going to her party. With or without him.

Begrudgingly, he agreed to go. Maybe he was feeling generous, or he could tell I was at the end of my rope. I put on a cute, baby doll outfit. I pulled my old collar from the back of the drawer—the black band with a little cute heart in the center. We met Ophelia and her crew at a bar in Brooklyn. The second I saw everyone, a warmth flooded my body. I felt like *myself* again.

Shawn, to his credit, played his old role as my Dominant. For a night, it felt like, maybe, we could be this again. I sat on his lap. When we took a group picture, he put his hand on my throat. I felt safe and kept and *his*.

"It's so fucking good to see you two," Ophelia said. We ended the night at the Seekers' Club. The night was winding down, and a half-devoured cake sat on the once-spanking-bench, now-makeshift-table between us.

"We miss you at the club," Carver added.

Shawn snorted. "That freak show? No thank you."

Immediately, my heart sank. *No*, I wanted to beg, *please. Keep your mouth shut. Just a little longer.*

Like Cinderella, begging her fairy godmother for another minute in those glass slippers.

"The fuck does that mean?" Ophelia asked. Her voice had knives in it.

Shawn shrugged. "C'mon. This place is like…adult fairy-tale land. We've got guys in baby diapers. Girls with dog leashes. Doesn't anyone else think it's kinda fucking weird that you're so afraid of real life, that you spend every Friday playing sexy freak show?"

The group suddenly went quiet. I felt like I was standing on a sheet of ice over a pond and I could feel the first, sickening crack under my feet.

"Get out," Ophelia said.

Shawn rolled his eyes. "Whatever."

"*Whatever?* Fuck you! You're not going to come here and insult my community on my fucking birthday! Get the fuck out of here!"

"Fine by me. I've been ready to go since we got here." He grabbed his jacket and then motioned for me. "Dove. C'mon."

But I froze.

Sitting next to me: Ophelia. My friends. My community.

On the other hand: Shawn. His arm outstretched. Watching me expectantly.

His eyes grew wide when I didn't move. "Oh, shit," he said. "Are we really doing this? Okay. Fuck it. Your call. The freaks or me."

My heart hammered in my throat. My vision blurred and I couldn't see anything. I sucked in a breath, and my body moved as if pulled by puppet strings, rising towards *him*—

* * *

Eh. You know what? Let's talk about that later.

The whole thing is embarrassing. It was a fucked-up night, is my point.

That night, I turned my back on my friends and my community. For a *man*, of all things.

I laid awake all that night and the next morning, staring at the ceiling, hollowed out.

Shawn slept well through noon the next day. Eventually, I rose from our bed. I shuffled into the kitchen, poured myself a bowl of cereal, and sat at the table, watching the pieces get wet and soggy in the milk.

I put my phone on the table and started scrolling. I had a notification from the Seekers Club app.

THE SEEKERS CLUB

Membership Revoked: Shawn H.

A surge of adrenaline shot through my veins.

Shawn had been banned from the club. And now, I was certain, I was next.

Suddenly, I was six again. My family was cleaved apart, my twin gone, and I felt like parts of me at been amputated, my tongue cut out, all because I'd reached for the wrong person.

What have I done? What have I done?

I pushed my thumb into the phone screen and deleted the app. If I saw my name pop up in the notifications, I was going to be sick.

"Dove?" Shawn's voice. Calling me back to bed.

I swallowed. My mouth was thick with saliva. My heart felt like a fist punching through my chest.

"I'm going to get coffee," I called back, doing everything in my power to make my voice sound *normal.* "Want some?"

"Yeah. Sure."

"Be right back."

But I wasn't.

I grabbed my keys and didn't look back.

I went straight to Ophelia's apartment. By time I knocked on the door, my eyes were already heavy with tears and I was doing everything in my power to keep them from spilling over.

She opened the door, standing there in a loose shirt and boy shorts, looking half-asleep herself. Her frizzy hair was an explosion around her head. When she saw me, her eyebrows pulled into a concerned furrow. "You okay?"

"I'm…"

Sorry. But I couldn't get the words out. It didn't feel like enough.

Nothing felt like enough. My throat was tight with the guilt and shame of it all.

"I fucked up," I said. My voice shook. "Really badly. I know I did. It's my fault and I can…I can survive it…but not if I don't have you. Not if I don't have my sister."

I didn't deserve her forgiveness. I didn't deserve her friendship. I waited for her to push me away, to call me out for being a push-over and a coward.

Instead, her expression softened. She stepped into the hall and put her arm around me.

She smelled like warm sheets. I choked back a sob.

"You'll never lose me," she said. "Especially not over some fucking man. C'mon in. I'll put on some coffee."

5

THE DICK PIC THAT BROKE ME

DOVE. Then.

Ophelia let me stay with her. "Until I found my own place." I was a woman unmoored. I hadn't only lost my boyfriend—I'd lost myself. It was going to take months to pull myself back together. I couldn't bring myself to go back to the Seekers' Club. I was convinced that Shawn's outburst at Ophelia's party had ruined me in their eyes forever and I was probably on a black list somewhere. The community I'd worked so hard to build now cut off from me completely.

A couple days dragged into a week and then a month. I was surviving on the kindness of Ophelia and a lot of comfort cheese. I couldn't play. I couldn't paint. It was like someone had sucked all the joy out of the world.

I wasn't comfortable in my own body. So I reinvented. I let my natural auburn hair grow back out and, as soon as it bobbed around my ears, I cut off any last traces of blonde. Ophelia suggested we get matching tattoos, so we did—she got a dove on her shoulder and I got a sprig of rosemary up

44

the back of my arm, one of Ophelia's flowers from Hamlet. It's true what they say about tattoos—once you get one, you're hooked. It wasn't as good as the pain I got from my Friday night spankings at the Club, but the jab of a needle lacing through my skin made me grit my teeth in a way that I liked when I was in need of a fix. I got a job at a cheese shop to supplement the income I'd lost from my lack of new paintings. I stopped looking at apartments when Ophelia and I decided we were better together than apart.

I still couldn't bring myself to join Ophelia on her Friday night ventures to the club. But every now and then, I got *the itch.*

It was a sticky, sweaty night in July when I finally re-downloaded the Seekers' App. Our AC was out and I was lying couch, reading *Damaged Hearts* for the thousandth time while Ophelia did her makeup across from me, getting ready for the Club.

"You should come out tonight," she said. "Lady Nine is doing a wax play demo. Should be fun."

"Cool." I turned the page. Poe was spitting between Quinn's legs and calling her filthy names. There was probably something wrong with me, that I could read this much smut with a straight face.

I felt Ophelia's eyes on me. "*Plus*, they have AC."

With my shirt sticking to my pits and a waterfall of sweat under my boobs, that should've closed the deal for me. Instead, I said, "Maybe next time."

"Well, if you're staying in all night, earn your keep." Ophelia pointed to a jar of paint that'd been sitting in the corner for a week. "The walls are fucked up. You can start repainting them."

"Shouldn't the landlord do that?"

"This place is rent controlled, baby. The landlord doesn't do *shit.*"

"I'll touch it up," I said. "Cross my heart."

But when Ophelia left, it felt hard to get off the couch, let alone paint. I forced myself to go through the motions—I taped down the corners and covered the floor in newspaper. Spud watched me from his spot in front of the rotating fan. Ophelia's dog—a well-fed tan French bulldog—was melted like a clock in a Dali painting, his tongue lolling out onto the floor. The apartment was old, and our long living room wall had splintered in places, the paint cracking. Ophelia had picked a watered down coral pink and I managed to apply the first layer before I found myself lying on my back on the floor side-by-side with Spud, the fan fluttering my hair and cooling the sweat stains on my shirt.

Half high from paint fumes, I couldn't stop thinking about the Club. Ophelia was there. My old friends were there. Right now. Playing. Without me. The FOMO was eating me up inside. I was delirious enough to think that maybe, *maybe*, they'd forgotten all about how I'd betrayed them the night of Ophelia's party.

I picked up my phone, found the Seekers Club app, and hit "download." My heart was racing as the app slowly came back to life on my phone. The logo of crisscrossed keys illuminated and I clicked it. I logged into my old account and, to my surprise, it let me back in.

My membership hadn't been revoked, after all.

I turned on the Seekers' App and found myself staring face-to-face with a woman I didn't recognize. My profile picture was me in my Shawn-era. Soft face. Submissive. Ready to please.

Just the sight of this version of me made my stomach twist.

My profile still read: Claimed by @heyitsshawn.

But the link didn't go anywhere. His profile was gone, removed from the app.

Meanwhile, I had to live with the ghost-of-Dove-past.

The more I stared the image of my old self, the grief inside of me melted into a hot, flaming rage.

Fuck him. Fuck Shawn. Fuck every dominant who ever thought he owned me. Fuck all men. Arrogant, entitled, soul-crushing fucking men—

In a rage, I deleted my old pictures; the pictures of *Shawn-era* me—skin with no tattoos, bleached blonde hair, and a thin black collar with the little pink heart around my throat in every photo. I tossed my natural dark hair which had finally grown out enough to graze my shoulders, gave the camera what Ophelia called my "fuck me" eyes, and took a selfie that showed off the colorful array of tattoos that ran up my right arm. With that, I changed my status from "claimed" to "seeking."

But there was one more change I had to make.

I'd labeled myself as a "submissive." I flicked through the options. "Switch" meant I could be either submissive or Dominant. "Masochistic" marked me as someone who enjoyed receiving pain—no thank you, I'd gotten enough of that with Shawn. "Sadist" meant that I enjoyed giving pain.

I needed to change my life. In a big way.

No more Misses-Nice-Doormat-Dove.

Maybe it *would* be therapeutic to make a grown man crawl to me.

Middle-aged men got Corvettes when they went through a crisis. I didn't want a car. I wanted some arrogant, cheeky, selfish boy to break for me. I wanted to make a grown man cry. I wanted him to crawl to me on his hands and knees and beg for my mercy—and then I wanted to deny him.

I wanted to make a man feel as small and helpless as Shawn had made me feel.

I changed my identity to "Dominant/Domme" and hit "save."

Minutes later, I got a message. *DoriNYC.*

> DORINYC
>
> how are you?

Well. That was fast.

I typed out: "Good! How's it going?" and then promptly deleted it. I had to ignore my instincts to reply enthusiastically with excessive exclamation points.

I remembered the Doms of my past. They'd all reeled me in the same way—they were cold and aloof, making me earn any scraps of affection.

So I played it cool.

> ME
>
> Fine.

Done. Send.

I could feel myself starting to sweat. Being standoffish was so unnatural to me that my pits were crying.

Hopefully, he was sweating, too. He replied back:

> DORINYC
>
> I like your profile. You're in the city?

> ME
>
> yes.

I stared at the phone, waiting for his response. Finally, he came back with a message so direct, it took the breath out of my lungs:

> DORINYC
>
> I want you to fuck me like you hate me.

I signed out of the app, dimmed my phone, and tried to steady the pounding in my heart. What the fuck was that?

I'd gotten creepy messages from men before, sure, both

on this app and on "vanilla" or non-kink dating sites. Men who wanted me to send them dirty pictures or Doms who immediately started in with *who's my good girl?*

But to *solicit* me? To dominate *him?*

I heard Shawn's voice in my ear: *what a freak. What an absolute, fucking freak.*

I silenced my notifications. I tried to put it out of my mind, but all night and all the next day, I couldn't stop thinking about his offer.

Well. Okay. Buuut what if...?

What if I could unleash a little rage, reclaim myself, all with someone who *wanted* me to be mean to him?

Tipsy, cozy with Spud flopped beside me, I felt primed to make bad decisions. I re-opened the Seekers' app. I went to my messages, where I'd left him on read. I'd gotten twenty more requests from people searching for a domme, but none of them were as bizarre or interesting as *DoriNYC.* I muted them. I clicked on his profile and started investigating.

DoriNYC.

Location: New York City

Age: 36

Pronouns: He/him

Seeking: A domme.

His profile image was semi-anonymous. It was a picture of his face from the nose-down. He was a conventionally attractive white boy, so—already—he had a face I'd like to punch. This, I figured, would make it easier for me to slap him and enjoy it. His profile image showed a trimmed, dark beard and a nice smile.

I was so used to the hardened, too-cool scowls of dominant men on these apps. I liked his smile. It was attractive. There was something familiar about him. I couldn't put my finger on it. But there was the nagging feeling like I'd seen him before—a face from a dream.

I scrolled through his public photos. You could add up to ten. He only had three. The first was his profile image. The second image showed more of him—he was sprawled in a chair, dressed trendy-casual (a t-shirt stretched across a broad chest, slacks fitted on a trim waist). His face was, again, hidden, but this time he held a book to his face—Stephen King's *It*—and had positioned the book so that it looked like the creepy, red-smiling clown face was his own. Points for creativity.

The last photo was the obligatory, kinky thirst trap. Taken in front of the mirror, maybe in his personal bathroom or at work, it was hard to say. He'd removed his shirt, showing off an impressively toned body underneath. Not built the way a gym-rat was built, but *fit*, svelte. His arms were toned, with a lovely, masculine dusting of dark hair. His head was bowed so you could only see his dark, curly hair, once again hiding his face. His arms were straight out in front of him, hands planted on either side of the sink.

Normally, this wouldn't be my type. *At all.* I was a submissive, after all. I liked my men tall, strong, and alpha. The Phantoms. The Carvers. The Poes. I liked them with a belt around their fists, a swagger in their stance, that *don't make me come over there and teach you a lesson* look in their eyes.

But even I had to admit—there was something about his last picture that drew me in. Something about the way his hands were splayed wide and fixed on the surface, giving the impression that he wouldn't move them, wouldn't budge, without direct permission.

Submissive, not in the roll over, belly up, wave the white flag in surrender way. But *submissive* the way the early humans must have felt when the first vicious wolf laid down at their feet—*oh. The beast has chosen me.*

Not gonna lie, it was kind of a turn on.

At that moment, his little green dot blinked on. He was online.

Looked like I wasn't the only lonely night owl on this app, *actively seeking*.

Spud engaged in such a good stretch, it made his whole-body shudder. I scratched his belly and, as he melted into my pets with a rattling grunt of affirmation, I considered my next move.

I reminded myself: I had the control here. The next steps were all up to me.

I messaged him back:

ME

Tell me more.

Almost immediately, he responded.

DORINYC

What do you want to know?

ME

Do you mean it? Or are you being dramatic?

DORINYC

I mean it.

I thought about *Damaged Hearts*. I didn't want to be Quinn—confused, lost, hungry for love.

I wanted to be Poe.

So I sent back:

ME

Tell me what you want. Don't leave anything out.

* * *

We talked all night. And then the next day. And on and on for weeks.

I found my mood would skyrocket any time my phone vibrated in my pocket. Dorian was incredibly vocal about what he wanted. We spent weeks messaging back and forth. We went over likes. Dislikes. What was his pain tolerance? He could take it. Slapping and hitting was good. I could hit him anywhere—his body, between the legs, on his face.

Choking, yes.

Scratching, yes.

Spanking, yes.

Could I leave marks? God, yes, please.

Dorian, apparently, never slept, because I'd fall asleep messaging him and then wake up to messages like:

DORINYC

What are your hard limits?

ME

What are yours?

I asked you first.

Yet I'm in charge, so…

Fine. Hard limits include scat, incest roleplay, knives, and permanent marks or branding.

Your turn.

I stared at his list. I sent back:

ME

Ditto.

DORINYC

Seriously? Nothing else is off the table for you?

Let me think about it.

And I did. I thought about it.

I wanted to give him my list of hard limits—things I wouldn't do in a scene. But as soon as I tried to think of something I wouldn't do, my brain hit a wall. It was like it physically wouldn't *let* me have hard limits.

I'd spent so long saying *yes* to everything Shawn wanted me to do, my tongue tied itself up in knots around the word *no*.

I bitched about it to Ophelia. She was half dressed, getting ready for a night out at the Seekers Club. As she drew a swooping cat eye, she said, "You could come with me to the club tonight. Get some ideas."

"Yeah…pass. But thank you."

Ophelia sighed. "Look, hard limits are easy. Just think of the shit you really don't want to do."

"Well, yeah. I know *that*. But it's like…okay. I can tell him hard limit, don't shit on my chest. But that's not really what I care about."

Her eyes flickered from the mirror to me. "You don't care if he shits on your chest?"

"I mean, *I do*. But I care more about my emotional boundaries. I just…I don't want to end up with a Shawn again."

Ophelia cocked her head. "So say that. You're the domme. You're in charge, D. You make the rules."

I made the rules. She was right. And it was time for me to be clear and precise about my boundaries and my limits.

I took out my phone, pulled up the Seekers' Club app, and spoke into it, letting the app translate my words into text. "Hard limit," I said. "Emotional manipulation. Say what you mean and mean what you say. Don't try to twist my feelings against me. I don't want to engage in a scene with you only to find that you hate it and you resent me for it later."

I re-read it, and then hit *send*. Ophelia pointed at me with her makeup brush. "Now *that*," she said, "is hot."

Ophelia left for the club. I cuddled up with Spud and opened a bottle of wine. Halfway through the bottle, I thought of another one.

ME

Hard limit: gaslighting. If I'm trying to express how I feel, listen to me. Acknowledge my feelings. Don't try to rewrite my narrative to match your own.

And another glass of wine in…

ME

Hard limit: man babies. I am not your mother. I won't coddle you. I won't do your laundry. I won't do your dishes.

I spent the night venting. It felt cathartic to get all my "hard limits" out. It wasn't until I finally crashed out in bed that my phone buzzed back.

DORINYC

Read and received. I'll respect your limits.

It's a good list. Makes me want to rethink mine.

ME

Update your limits at any time.

Let's make this a changing thing.

And the next day, he took me up on that.

DORINYC

Hard limit: people who don't use the Oxford comma.

That made me grin. It became a running language between us. Every now and then at random, one of us would send a new limit.

> **ME**
>
> Hard limit: cutting in line.

> **DoriNYC**
>
> Hard limit: dog earing pages instead of using a book mark.

> **ME**
>
> Hard limit: Men in their twenties.

> **DORINYC**
>
> Hard limit: strollers in bars.

> **ME**
>
> Hard limit: Leaving one slice of cheese on the plate.

I was growing. Changing. Learning how to communicate in a way that felt fun and flirty and *good*.

Meanwhile, Ophelia had picked up a show. Off, *off* Broadway, but I was insanely proud of her. When she wasn't busting her ass at rehearsal, we decompressed together, curled up on the couch with a too-large bowl of microwave popcorn, re-watching comfort movies.

"Okay, sexy Jeff Goldblum or nerdy Jeff Goldblum?" Ophelia asked. Spud snored loudly between us as she scrolled through the options on the TV.

"I feel like you just said the same thing twice." I popped a kernel of popcorn in my mouth.

"I'll rephrase. Dinosaurs or giant bugs?"

"Dinosaurs. Definitely."

My phone buzzed in my pocket. I shifted on the couch to check it.

DORINYC

Hard limit: Chinese takeout with no duck
sauce.

I felt a grin crawling up my lips.

ME

Rookie mistake. You need a sauce drawer.

DORINYC

I'm afraid to ask.

A sauce drawer.

I said what I said.

As in a drawer for sauce?

Hold please.

I set the bowl of popcorn down, got up, and moved into the kitchen. I pulled out a drawer that was filled with extra sauce packets—ketchup, mustard, soy sauce, hot sauce, orange sauce, duck sauce. You name it, we had it.

I lifted my phone and snapped a picture.

"What're you doing?" Ophelia asked from underneath the blanket-pile.

"Taking a picture of our sauce drawer for Dorian."

"Huh," she said.

It was one of those layered *huhs*. A *huh* that was holding back.

I squinted at her. "What?"

Ophelia shrugged. "Nothing. It's just cute how much you two message. He's growing on you."

I scoffed. "Yeah. Like mold."

Another dubious *uh-huh* from the couch.

I added, "He's my emotional support, self-loathing cis man."

"Word to that. So are you going to squeeze hot sauce on him or something?"

"Oh, no, we were just…talking."

Hearing it out loud, I realized what Ophelia was saying. She was right. I was supposed to be dominating him. Instead, I was…*getting comfortable.*

Too comfortable.

And we all know how badly things ended when I got comfortable.

Head in the game, Dove.

My phone buzzed again.

DORINYC

You were correct. That's a sauce drawer.

You're either brilliant or insane.

I pressed my lips together. I turned on my *Domme Dove* voice.

ME

Is that any way to talk to your mistress?

DORINYC

You're either brilliant or insane…ma'am.

What a little brat. I left him on read and snuggled back up with Ophelia. We watched the rest of the movie and ate our big bowl of popcorn until it was nothing but kernels. Ophelia said goodnight, and she and Spud shuffled into her room, closing the door.

I went to my room and crawled into bed, but I couldn't sleep.

I tried my favorite coping mechanism. I pulled my

battered copy of *Damaged Hearts* off the shelf and turned to a well-worn section—chapter fifteen:

The little bell above the door jingled as I burst into Poe's record shop.

The sound startled Behemoth, who leapt off a shelf with a yowl. The black cat scurried out of the room, shooting me a glare as it went.

Even the cat didn't want me here.

"We're closed," Poe's voice called out.

He was standing in front of a box of records, sorting through them.

I stood there. Staring at him. Soaked with rain and dripping onto his floor. When he saw me, his jaw tightened. Quickly, his eyes dropped back down to the records. His fingers moved, still sorting, but I could tell he was doing it blindly, flipping through the sleeves too quickly.

"Quinn." My name was hard and cold on his tongue now. Our fight had sucked all the warmth out of it. "I told you to stay away."

"Look at me." I closed the space between us. He shifted away, moving his eyes to the floor. Anger flushed hotly on my cheeks. "Look me in the eyes," I demanded, "and tell me you feel nothing."

His sharp eyes met mine. "Nothing?" he snapped. "Nothing? I wish I felt nothing! That's the point! I look at you and I feel everything! Hate. Shame. Guilt." He grabbed my chin, forcing me to hold his gaze when he spit out the word: "Disgust."

I swung my hand to slap him, but he grabbed my wrist before I could make contact. I struggled in his grip and we tumbled against the table, the boxes of records shuddering. His body pressed flushed against mine. My heart beat was pounding. This close, I could feel his breath beating against my face—the short, rapid breaths. Even though the denim of his jeans, his hard erection pressed against my hip.

A thin laugh escaped me. "Disgust? That certainly doesn't feel like disgust."

I rolled my hips against his. He sighed. "Quinn..." he warned.

My name was changing on his tongue now, the heat returning. His voice went tight with familiar longing. I gripped Poe's hips, feeling the bones underneath sharply against my palms, and grinded my body against his.

His beard prickled my cheek as he sighed into my ear. But it was his moan—a deep, uncontrolled sound that escaped him—that I loved the most.

"Go ahead," I hissed in his ear. "Show me how little you think of me."

He reached between us and unbuckled his belt. I gasped as he ripped it from his waist, the leather snapping.

"Give me your hands," he said.

I held my arms up towards him. He wound the belt around my wrists and threaded it together, pulling them tight. Locking me into place. His hands roved up my leg, under my skirt. He ripped off my panties and—

I closed the book. This was my favorite book. At my favorite part. And yet...I couldn't focus.

I glanced at my phone lying on the charger beside my bed.

I couldn't stop thinking about *him*.

Damaged Hearts was a good book. But Dorian was a *better* book, and I wanted to keep turning the pages.

I pulled up the Seekers' App. I sent him a message:

ME

Ready to be good?

A reply, almost immediately.

DORINYC

Absolutely not.

ME

That mouth is going to get you in trouble.

I certainly hope so.

I hesitated. But I was feeling bold, and horny, and—
Fuck it.
I sent him:

ME

How hard are you right now?

I stared at the screen, feeling my heart flutter in my chest as he typed out his reply.

DORINYC

You've turned me into Pavlov's dog.

Every time my phone buzzes, I get hard.

ME

Ah. So he IS trainable.

In the right hands.

I opened the camera app on my phone. I rested a hand on my chest, adjusted the camera, and snapped a picture. The picture showed me from the neck down. I was in a thin night shirt and the neck went down low enough that it exposed the swell of my breasts.
I sent him the picture and replied:

ME

These hands?

A lengthy pause, before he sent back:

DORINYC

Those will do.

Question.

ME

Go ahead.

What's your comfort level with dirty talk?

I'm comfortable with it.

I enjoy it. Immensely. The written word is the
height of erotic expression, in my opinion.

What do you want to hear?

Degrade me. Call me a bastard. Pathetic.
Desperate. Get creative.

Is there anything you don't like, my
desperate, pathetic bastard?

I don't particularly like small dick humiliation.

Of course. Men and their penises. I almost rolled my eyes.

ME

Got a complex, Tiny Tim?

DORINYC

I just don't like being lied to.

What a fucking arrogant asshole. I couldn't help the
smirk that emerged on my lips.

ME

Prove it.

DORINYC

Permission to send a NSFW pic?

My heart picked up a beat in my chest. Was I about to get a dick pic? More than that...did I actually *want* to see it?

Honestly? Yeah. Kinda. Curiosity got the better of me, and I sent:

ME

Permission granted.

He sent it, and my phone tumbled right out of my hands, bouncing on my knee and hitting the mattress. I scrambled to get it, snatching it up, and stared at the picture in front of me.

Jesus. He was hung.

The picture captured Dorian from the waist down. It looked like he was lying in bed on top of a deep blue duvet. Grey boxer briefs hugged his strong thighs. I could easily make out the outline of his monster cock. His erection lifted the grey fabric, casting a shadow underneath it.

My mouth went wet with want. It was the kind of cock I wanted to get on my knees for, trace with my tongue, and pull deep into my throat—

No. *No.* I had to get out of a submissive head-space.

I wasn't the one worshipping him. He was the one worshipping *me.*

What would badass, femdom Dove do?

I texted back:

ME

Is that you right now?

DORINYC

Yes.

Talking to me gets you that hard?

Also, yes.

> Do you want to stroke it?

Yes.

> Yes…?

Yes, ma'am.

> Go ahead. Give me proof that you're obeying.

There was a brief pause in communication, and then I got the notification. Dorian sent a voice note. *Did I want to play it?* A thread of pleasure pulled through me even at the sight of it. My wireless ear phones were charging on the bedside table. I plugged them in, synced them to my phone, and hit *play*.

Immediately, sounds of Dorian's bedroom filled my ears. The rustling sounds of a busy hand. And then…a low, deep moan. Followed by something choked. Swallowing back a whimper.

Oh, fuck.

The sounds of his frustrated pleasure sent a rush through me.

ME

> Is that the best you can do? Stroke it like you mean it.

DORINYC

Are you touching yourself?

I bit my lip. This was my chance to have fun with him.

ME

> To you? Absolutely not. I'm bored.

> I might just fall asleep and leave you stroking all night.

Another voice note. I could hear him panting in this one. At the end, he let out a strained, *"Fuck..."*

His voice! I could hear his voice for the first time. It was dark. Deep. Masculine. Like the first sip of a strong cup of coffee in the morning. I could hear the ache in it. The way he was all twisted up. *For me.*

> ME
>
> Are you close?

DORINYC

Yes.

> Already? So desperate. We're going to have to work on your stamina.

Yes, mistress.

What a good boy he was being. Amazing how all the brat died from his tongue when he wanted something.

Time to teach him a lesson.

> ME
>
> Too bad. Don't cum.

I could see him typing. Then the three dots disappeared. They came back again and disappeared again.

I grinned. Aw. He was fighting with himself. How cute.

Is he trying not to beg right now?

I slipped my hand into my panties. I needed to relieve the pressure knotting between my legs. I found myself swollen and slippery beyond belief.

Finally, he managed to text:

DORINYC

Please.

ME

> Please what? We're going to train you how to beg better than that, pup.

More typing, deleting, and typing again.

Was I being too mean?

I bit my lip. Hold up. Was I good at this?

Fuck, I was good at this. More than that. *I was enjoying this.*

I was having way too much fun tormenting this poor guy.

My efforts were reaffirmed when my phone pinged again. Another voice note.

I turned up the volume and hit play.

Light, thready breathing.

"Please, mistress…" *Dear fucking God, the growl of his voice was an aphrodisiac.* "Please, let me cum…fuck, I'm—" A sound escaped him—this low, frustrated whimper. The sound of something feral quickly unraveling. It sent a shudder through me, my nipples hardening into tight knots under my shirt. He continued to narrate, his voice strained: "I'm dripping down my stomach. You've officially made me insane with desire. Every stroke makes me—mm." His breath hitched. I imagined his hand sliding up his cock, curling around that sensitive head. "Makes me lose a little more control. I don't think I can hold back…much longer…"

Holy *fuck*. That wasn't begging. That was poetry. His sweet moans, the heavy, thick desperation in his voice…the way his breath caught every time he hit a sweet spot.

I replayed the message again, but this time I stretched out and slid my fingers underneath my waistband. I was soaked. Completely.

The ache was borderline unbearable. It was time to do something about that.

I reached into my bedside drawer. I pulled out my

favorite toy—a magic wand with a heavy-duty, vibrating head. I took off my panties, propped the phone on the table beside me, and nestled the toy between my legs. Then I reached over and hit *record a voice note.*

"Don't touch," I told him. "Just listen."

I flipped on the vibrator. I was so turned on, even the low level vibrations sent pleasure whipping through me. I didn't hold back—I turned it up. I moaned into it, allowing myself to enjoy the sweet hum of the toy against my sensitive, swollen clit. My legs closed around it and I tilted my head back, closing my eyes.

"It's too bad you're such a brat," I told him. I could hear the breathiness in my voice as I arched against the toy, softly riding it. "If you were a good boy...you might be here. Worshipping my pussy with your good-boy tongue. Instead, you're all alone...gripping your sheets...leaking...aching...as you get to listen to this toy make me feel..." A jolt of pleasure made me gasp. "So...fucking...good..."

I teased myself, rolling the vibrating head over my slippery slit. I let myself moan and whimper and *enjoy it* for a full minute before I paused to hit *send.*

I waited for him to listen to the voice note. He came back with:

DORINYC

I'm making that my fucking ring tone.

I couldn't help the laugh that escaped me. A laugh that quickly turned into a moan.

God. I'd hardly started playing myself and, already, I was so close.

Maybe I really was enjoying this domination thing more than I realized.

I hit *record* again. I massaged the vibrator between my legs. "Go ahead," I said. "Take your cock in your hand. Stroke it. Stroke it just how you like it. And then…when you can't take it anymore…push yourself further." I bit my lip. My legs were shaking around the vibrator, the image of him struggling against his hand almost pushing me over the edge. A whine escaped me. The pleasure was making me dizzy, building, threatening to burst…and I finally relented.

"Cum, pet. Now. Let me hear you."

I cut the vibrations. Even after I turned the toy off, my cunt was still buzzing, hanging on the edge. I hit *send* and waited for his reply.

A *ping*. Another voice note.

I hit *play* at the same time I pushed the button on the vibrator. It sprung back to life, immediately making my eyes roll back. My heels dug into my mattress. I closed my eyes and saw *him*. Working himself over in his bed. That scruffy jaw tilted back. Those full lips parted in a moan. The muscles in his arm working. The grip of that strong, large hand as it slid up and down his dripping monster cock. He sounded so close—as though he were right in the bed beside me. Stroking himself. Panting in my ear. I heard his breath get quick. Then quicker. He let out a low curse: "Oh, *fuck, Dove*—"

My vibrator buzzed mercilessly right up against my clit. I shouted as I came with him, my hips lifting off the bed. My body burst with hard, tight pulses. I thrashed with pleasure, rolling onto my stomach, and I found myself riding the vibrator.

I put his voice note on repeat. I listened to the way he moaned my name over and over as I came a second time, and then a third. Drooling into my pillow. Rocking against the sweet buzzing buddy until I was aching with the pleasure of it all.

I turned off the vibrator and tossed it aside. I caught my breath. Spots of light danced in front of my vision. My phone was still replaying Dorian's moans as he came until I finally pulled myself together enough to tap the screen, silencing him.

Christ. Had I ever come that hard before?

Definitely not in the past year.

Definitely not with Shawn.

My phone blinked. One unread message. I clicked it open.

DORINYC

Thank you, mistress.

His message was followed by a single black heart.

Why did that stupid emoji make my heart flip?

It's not him. You're not getting feelings for a bratty submissive. You're just fluttering because you came, like, three times in a row.

This man's dirty talk game has got you dick-matized.

Still, it was *nice*. This felt nice.

When was when it occurred to me:

I'm the domme now. We just had a scene. Our first, real scene. I needed to provide aftercare.

I rolled onto my stomach, cradled my phone to my chest, and immediately started texting.

ME

How are you feeling?

DORINYC

Spent.

Emotionally.

That drew a pause from him. For a minute, I was worried that I'd pushed him too far. Maybe he was in bed, breaking down right now, and I wasn't there to pick his pieces back up. Guilt pinched at my chest. Finally, he replied with—

DORINYC

Happy.

A tingling relief swept through me. I grinned—this stupid, huge grin. Feeling bolder than ever, I sent:

ME

I think it's time we meet.

DORINYC

I was thinking the same. Just tell me when and where.

I thought about it. The Seekers' Club was the smart choice. It was a public setting in case Dorian turned out to be a freak, but they had private rooms. We could have our own space.

But…that would mean I'd have to go back to the club. I'd have to look those people in the eyes. The people I'd hurt last winter. I'd have to explain to them that the reason I hadn't been to the club is because I couldn't face them, and because I didn't know if they'd even like the woman I was now—this different version of myself.

So instead I said:

ME

Do you know Cure? It's a wine bar downtown.

DORINYC

I know it.

Friday. At seven. Don't be late.

If I am, will you punish me?

Don't tempt me.

> But mistress, tempting you is the whole point.

I snorted on a laugh.

> ME
> Be good.

> DORINYC
> I'm incapable.

> You'll learn.

> Yes, mistress.

I typed in the word *goodnight* and put a red heart emoji at the end. But my thumb hovered over the *send* button.

Don't. Don't do this. Isn't this the same thing you did with Shawn? You trust too easy. You fall too easy.

Don't be easy.

I bit my lip. I deleted the drafted text, closed out of the app, and darkened my phone, ending the conversation. I put up my phone and rolled over in bed, closing my eyes and letting the thrill of the night wash through my body, lapping at me like gentle waves.

* * *

Friday came, and I was so nervous, I thought I might throw up on the subway. It was one thing to dominant him from behind the screen—but what if I couldn't do it in person? What if I royally messed this up and shattered the fantasy for both of us?

I had to get it right. This was serious business. It felt somewhere between a first date and a job interview. It was summer in the city, and I had dressed in army green cargo

70

shorts, boots, and a threw on a loose, light blouse. I felt like Dr. Ellie Sattler from Jurassic Park, which is to say: I felt powerful.

I liked Cure, but mostly, for the proximity to my work —*Cheese Louise*, a mom-and-pop fromagerie. The cheese shop was right across the street, so I could get off work and immediately unwind with a glass of wine. It was also mid-level, classy place, with dim lights and dark velvet walls.

A woman greeted me at the door and gave me a small table by the window. I was there before Dorian. Already, he was getting himself in trouble. But where his tardiness would've royally pissed me off if this was a *date*, date, instead, I found myself tingling at the possibility of punishing him.

Finally, the door opened. My breath caught in my throat.

Was that him? Dorian. In the flesh. Real. Breathing. *Alive.* The man in front of me wore dark, creaseless slacks. A patterned button up. He had dark eyes and a smooth, short beard that outlined the sharpness of his jaw. Thick back hair that rose to wild curls at the top of his head and tapered off around his ears.

He looked similar enough to the half-hidden man in the photos. But he didn't *carry himself* like a submissive—nothing about him was shy. He strode in with confidence, his eyebrows furrowed, almost annoyed. As though he lived here, and was irritated to find that a swarm of people had suddenly invaded his space.

I knew for sure it was him when his eyes caught mine and that intense frown broke with the smallest hint of a smile.

It was the smile I recognized. That tight-lipped, contained smile. Slightly crooked, as though he were trying hard to keep himself from enjoying life *too* much.

There was my Dorian.

He approached my table and his hand touched the back of his chair.

"You're here," he said. His voice—that same voice that begged and whimpered over the voice notes. Not too dark and deep, but level, precise, each word crisp and articulated.

He sounded surprised, as though he hadn't been certain I would show up.

"I'm here," I repeated his words back to him. I cocked my head. "And you are…" I checked my phone. "Ten minutes late."

"Work ran late." He remained there, standing, and I realized then that he was waiting for permission. My permission.

I was in charge here. I had to keep reminding myself of that.

I nodded to the chair. "Sit."

He did, settling in. He rested his hands on the table, clasping a wrist. The waitress fluttered over—the woman who hadn't had time to serve me before, now seemed to have her whole day open up for the attractive man across from me.

"What are you having?" he asked me.

"Mojito," I said.

"Make it two," he said, and handed the drink list back to the waitress.

I watched and realized, then, how fucking strange this was.

I'd heard this man *absolutely unravel* for me only nights ago.

And now, for the first time, I was meeting him. Face to face.

A strange shyness crept over me. "So," I asked to break the ice, "where do you work?"

His eyes met mine. And I noticed them now—really noticed them. Not just the color of them—robin egg blue. It was the *clarity* of them. The sharpness. He looked at you and you could tell he wasn't conjuring the next thing he wanted to say in his head. He was *seeing* you. Really seeing you. Watching you with intelligent, deliberate focus.

I found it both exciting and deeply unsettling. Like I was on an autopsy table and he was peeling back layers of skin, hunting dispassionately around my insides, weighing and measuring my heart.

"Are we really doing this?" he asked me.

I blinked. "Doing what?"

"Vanilla small talk."

That spun my head around. Here was a man the opposite of Shawn. Shawn had wanted only vanilla—the appearance of what he deemed *correct* and *normal*.

Dorian had no interest in my job, my friends, my home life. He just wanted me to step on his throat and made him whimper.

And that was what *I* wanted too, wasn't it? All the kinky play. No strings attached. But now that we were here—face to face—I found myself curious about the man behind the username.

"Does it hurt?" I asked him. "Is small talk painful for you?"

"Incredibly."

"Good thing you're a masochist, then, because we're about to make the tiniest fucking talk."

I traced my fingers around the condescension of my glass, stroking the wet cold. The air had shifted between us, taut and tense. He seemed to read into my silence, because the muscle in his jaw flexed briefly, and I saw the moment he decided to give in. He checked his watch—a real, actual wrist watch—and then relented with: "Alright. I have an idea."

"I'm listening."

"We'll play a game. For five minute, we'll take turns asking rapid fire questions about each other. Don't think. Just answer. Go."

Who was in control—me or him? But I couldn't deny that

I like a challenge, and more than that, I like a game, so his offer hit all my sweet spots.

I cocked my head. Challenge accepted. "Alright. But we're doing this right. I don't trust you not to cheat."

I pulled out my phone, set it face up on the table, and pulled up my clock app. I set the timer to five minutes.

He looked amused. "Wise of you."

"Starting...*now*." I hit the button. The clock started ticking. "Cats or dogs?"

"Cats." His gaze never disconnected from mine and he immediately sent a question back: "Your comfort meal?"

"Grilled cheese, extra grilled, with a side of more pickles than should be legal. Your perfect day?"

"A book, a beverage, and no one to bother me. What do you hate most in this world?"

"Seeing pretty men happy."

The edge of his mouth quirked upwards with surprise. "Are you calling me pretty?"

"You're not my type."

Which was—*technically*—true. He was *not* my type. My type was strong, brutish, and dominant. He was quick-tongued, librarian-chic, and submissive.

If he took offense, he didn't let it show. If anything, that answer seemed to please him.

I shot his question back at him: "What do *you* hate?"

"Cilantro."

He got a follow up, so I took one too: "Counter, what do you *love*?"

"My sister."

The answer seemed to surprise him the second it came out of his mouth. He blinked, then looked momentarily ashamed, and though he'd let too much of himself slip out.

He cleared his throat. "But that stays between us. I'll never hear the end of it."

I held up two fingers. "Scout's honor. Is she older or younger?"

"Younger."

"Do you have any other siblings—?"

"My family is off limits," he interrupted. His voice was dark suddenly. The mood had shifted, gone cold, like a winter's breeze.

I pressed my lips together. I swallowed my questions with a sip from my glass.

He shifted in his seat. He veered with: "Why do you enjoy domination?"

There it was. I knew the answer, the truth that thrummed against the back of my teeth. That I'd been dominated by too many bad men and I was sick of it. That Shawn had ruined it for me. That, like Quinn from the romance novel, I'd come to a point in my life when I needed a full, real change.

But those weren't things I was ready to confess to him.

Maybe we both had scars we weren't ready to show.

Instead, what came out of my mouth was: "I don't."

Dorian blinked. His head tilted like a confused dog. I could see the next question starting to form on his tongue but...

My phone rang. *Ding-a-ling-a-ling!*

I clicked the side buttons, silencing it. "Time is up." I told him. His lips thinned, and I could sense his disappointment. I lifted my eyebrows with faux confusion. "What?"

"I just...have more questions."

"Aw. You're the one who didn't want to get to know each other. Don't write checks you can't cash, baby girl." I tucked my phone away. "Now. I think we have to address the elephant in the room. You were late."

"By seven minutes," he reminded me.

I stretched forward. *Time to remind him who's in charge.* "So let's talk about your punishment."

Dorian, to his credit, didn't flinch or shy away. Instead, he held my gaze and said: "Alright."

Under the table, I used one foot to kick the boot off the other. "You're going to rub my feet."

His eyes briefly widened. "Here?"

"Right now." I slid my foot up his thigh and into his lap. I wiggled my toes. "Sock."

His gaze flitted around briefly, gauging to see if anyone noticed me going shoeless in a nice-ass wine bar. Then, underneath the table, he undressed my foot. "Nice clocks," he said, referring to the cute little illustrated clocks printed on my socks. He peeled my sock off so my bare heel rested in his lap.

I tapped it against his thigh. "Afraid of it?"

His eyes met mine. "No." He cradled my foot in his hand. Slowly, he began to press in.

Oh. This wasn't a soft, tickling rub. He was really going in. He cracked my toes. Kneaded the balls of my feet. When he dug his thumbs into the painful arch, I moaned.

His dark eyebrows furrowed. Angry. "Quiet."

I scoffed. Him? Giving *me* orders? "Excuse me?"

"You're making a scene," he complained.

"Don't worry, no one's looking at you. They're looking at me."

He jammed his thumb on the arch of my foot. A knot burst and pleasure exploded. I hiccupped on a gasp and I felt my cheeks flush.

Christ, this foot rub was going to get me off. Had it been that long since I'd been touched? Yeah. Eight months. I guess so.

I tried to refocus. I shot back: "Or are you just afraid someone you know is going to walk in and see you worshipping my feet like the little pet you are?"

No response from him. But when I stretched my leg out, I felt my heel brush against the hardness of him.

He loves it when I'm mean to him.

"That's enough," I said. "Re-sock me."

He did as he was told, wiggling my sock discreetly back up my ankle. I shoved my foot back in my boot and gave him the other foot, which he began to rub.

"Do you know what your problem is?" I told him.

"Tell me."

"I've dated a thousand men like you."

"A thousand?" he said dryly. "When do you have time to sleep?"

"Are you slut shamming me?"

"No, mistress."

I motioned towards him. "You're handsome. Privileged. You probably never had a bad day in your life. You've been handed everything on a silver platter…but you know, deep down, you don't deserve it. You don't deserve your fancy watch. You don't deserve your mother doting on you. You don't deserve the women who get on their knees and suck you without asking for anything in return, because they're just so *grateful* to be honored with your monster cock. How am I doing?"

He didn't answer. He just swallowed, and his Adam's apple bobbed, and I knew I'd hit a nerve.

Good. He was going to have to get used to being uncomfortable around me.

"Sock," I said. Gently, he nudged my sock back onto my feet.

He'd stopped bitching. Already, he was learning how to be obedient. I smiled.

"Don't worry, pretty boy. I'm here to set your karma right."

There it was. That shine in his eyes. An edge of hopefulness behind that dark cynicism. *He wanted to be punished.* This was a man who liked getting into trouble. I made a mental note to be careful with how much leash I gave him.

The boundaries were as much for his sake as for mine. The deeper our conversation went, the more I felt the ambient vibes of Cure melt around us until there was nothing but me, and Dorian, and his intense eyes, staring right through me. He was calm the whole evening. Collected. But there was this energy around him—a bit like being near a dog with a muzzle. He seemed capable of biting, and with the way the evening was going, I thought I might let him. I might enjoy punishing him for his teeth, too.

I might enjoy this all a bit *too much.*

We'd been sitting here—what? Twenty minutes? And neither of us had touched our drinks, the condensation soaking the napkins underneath.

"How's your drink?" I asked him pointedly.

A wry smile. "I have no idea."

Go ahead, Dove. Tell him what to do. He wants it.

"Drink," I demanded.

He lifted the thin glass to his mouth, tilted it, and started drinking.

It shouldn't be this erotic. The way his lips kissed the glass. Watching the hollow of his throat contract and expand with every swallow. His gaze still trained on me. I was so hypnotized, he was halfway through before I realized: he wasn't stopping. And he wouldn't. He was *chugging* the cocktail, all because I'd told him to drink.

Which felt a lot like: *yes, you're giving orders, but who's in control here, really?*

Little brat.

I frowned. "Stop."

He did. He took a deep breath. What was left was mostly ice.

He motioned to the bartender. "Another round, please."

We had a second cocktail. Then a third. The more we talked, the less I knew him. Apart from our rapid-fire interrogation, he was a master at dodging the personal questions. Meanwhile, I couldn't help myself. I started spilling as though it was my own personal therapy session. I told him about how come to New York to attend art school, but found breaking into mural art was harder than anticipated, and a lot of *knowing* the right people. I told him about my earliest trauma (parent's divorce). I told him about Ophelia and sprinkled in a few details of our adventures, all while never bringing up Shawn. Dorian stayed mostly quiet, listening, and occasionally interjecting to ask a question.

"What's your family like?" he asked.

The night was winding down and I could feel the alcohol rosying my cheeks. "I thought family was off limits."

"*My* family is off limits. I want to know about yours."

"I don't really know my dad. He left when I was six. My parents got divorced and it was...contentious, to say the least. I have a twin brother. Dad got my brother, mom got me. A clean split, I guess."

"That sounds traumatic."

I put my drink to my lips. "What doesn't kill us makes us weirder, right?"

"Do you keep in touch with your brother?"

"Sort of. We hated each other on principle for like...most of our lives. But we reconnected after college. Discovered we had more in common than we realized. He's come to visit a couple times—it's strange, getting to know your actual twin in your thirties. But...I don't know..."

I was rambling, and my tongue was starting to tie itself in knots.

I met his gaze, expecting that glazed over, bored look Shawn or my mother often got when I started talking about myself. Instead, those blue eyes were fixed on me. Unwavering.

"You don't know what?" he asked.

"I guess I feel like maybe it doesn't matter that we didn't spend our childhoods together. Like things happen when they're supposed to happen." I was talking too much. Heat was rising into my cheeks. I narrowed my eyes at Dorian. "Stop looking at me like that."

"Like what?"

"Like you're...actively listening to me. It's unnerving."

"You can blindfold me, if you'd like."

There he was—the same Dorian who propositioned me within minutes of messaging me. I was drawn to the way he fearlessly said the quiet things out loud. Like he wasn't afraid to *want*. It sent a finger of heat tickling down my body.

"What are your feelings?" I asked. "Thoughts? Hopes and dreams?"

"I'd like to meet up again," he said. "Once a week, preferably."

"And in these meet-ups, we'll play?"

"Yes. I don't want to be your boyfriend. Or your friend. I just want to be your dog." He paused for a moment, dropping into thought. "I want clear boundaries," he continued. "Our play sessions—and our lives—those are separate."

A little, nagging warning in my chest. "Are you married?"

"No. Are you?"

Was that a light of jealousy in his eyes?

I shook my head. His shoulders relaxed.

"But I don't care if you see other people," I told him. "Like you said. This isn't..."

"Romantic," he filled in.

The way those blue eyes held my gaze made me flutter.

Yes. Let's put up these boundaries.

"But," I added, "I'd rather you not play with anyone else."

He blinked. That response seemed to surprise him.

I continued, "If that's okay. I don't want anyone undoing my…hard work."

His back stiffened. I'd set him on edge, but I couldn't tell if it was in a *good* or *bad* way.

We were still learning each other, after all.

"I can agree to that," he said. "As long as you don't play with anyone else either."

"Fine."

"Great."

There was a strange electricity in negotiating with Dorian. Both of our tones had sharpened. Our eyes remained trained on each other, as though we were daring the other to blink.

The waitress came over with our bill.

"You going to get that?" I asked him.

Perks of being a domme, after all.

Didn't help that my checking account was only in the double-digits.

Dorian broke eye contact. He slid the bill in front of him and took out his wallet. I still had no idea what he did for a living, but the thin, leather wallet and the shine on his watch told me he probably lived comfortably enough that this wouldn't make a dent.

He walked me out to the street. He lifted his arm and let out a sharp whistle, hailing a cab. I was quietly charmed. Who whistled for a cab anymore? Most people just pushed a button on their phone. There was something old fashioned about it that I liked.

The cab rolled to a stop in front of us. He opened the door and gestured me inside.

I twisted around to face him. Standing close like this, I

noticed how tall he was. I had to tilt my head up to meet his gaze. "What's your address?" I asked.

His jaw tightened. "We've both been drinking. I don't think…"

"I'm not coming home with you. Not tonight. How are Fridays for you?"

"Open."

"Good. I'm coming over next Friday at seven." I walked my fingers over his chest. "Do you think you can control yourself between now and then?"

"How do you mean?"

"Don't come. Between now and Friday. I'll know."

His throat bobbed as he swallowed. "Yes, mistress."

"Good."

And then…I kissed him.

I hadn't planned on it. In fact, I'd told myself repeatedly that I *wouldn't*.

But my body moved forward instinctively, as though we'd been married for twenty years and this was just the way of things, a gentle kiss before we parted ways for the night. As though his soul recognized mine, he opened too, applying pressure. The heat of his mouth sought mine. He tasted like sweet liquor and white knuckled restraint.

I sealed the kiss without pulling away. Our bodies swayed, foreheads pressed together.

"Do you like kissing me?" I asked.

"Yes." He panted lightly against my mouth.

"Do you want to kiss me again?"

"Yes."

I ghosted my lips across his. The energy between us was electric, and I was buzzing on it.

"Then enjoy it…because that's the last time you'll feel my lips…until you prove to me that you can be a good boy."

I gave him a single, gentle kiss, and then pulled back. His

head tilted forward, lips hunting for mine. A small hum left him—a warning, the way a dog growls before it bites.

I thought about the beat of his breath over the voice notes. The gravel in his voice. The way he moaned: *I don't think I can hold back.*

This is what it's like to kiss a man who is constantly pulling on the leash of his self-control.

I put my fingers to his chest, stalling him.

As much fun as I was having…I didn't know his limits. I didn't know *him*. And I needed to slow us both down before I got myself into trouble.

I slid into the cab. I made room in the seat beside me. "There's room enough for two if you wanna share a ride."

He hung in the doorway, his long arms stretched over the top of the cab. Those blue eyes looked charged, vibrant in the dark.

"It's a nice night. I need to walk this off. Get home safe."

"You too."

He shut the door. I watched him step back onto the curb, shove his hands in his pockets, and start a quick walk down the city street.

In the rearview mirror, the cabbie lifted his eyebrows at me.

I grinned like a kid a Christmas. "I gave him a boner."

The cabbie gave me a thumbs up.

* * *

Ophelia wasn't there when I got back to the apartment. I walked Spud and, when we came back upstairs, I found myself staring at the half-finished wall.

Inspiration swept through me. I wanted to hold a paintbrush. I wanted to *create* something.

I took out my supplies from my room, dragged them into

83

the living room, and painting. Not the simple pink that Ophelia had picked up. Dark lines. Swirls. People and monsters.

It was almost two in the morning when Ophelia came home. I heard the door click behind her quietly, trying to stay silent in case I was asleep. Instead, I heard her step into the living room and stop when she spotted me drawing my brush across the wall.

"What're you doing?" she asked.

"Covering up the cracks."

I'd turned the wall into a mural. A woman swooped across the top section. Her hair ran trickling down. Underneath her, a creature pulled her hair into its mouth with sharp little claws. Eating her up.

Ophelia stood beside me, assessing the painting. Slowly, she nodded. "Fucking awesome."

I turned to her. I could feel smudges of paint drying on my cheek. "I'm meeting up with Dorian again on Friday. We're going to his place to play."

Her eyes met mine and a smile lit up her mouth. "You know what that means, right?" She knocked her hip against mine. "We're going shopping, Vincent van Gorgeous."

The next day, we went to a fetish store. And a lingerie store. I blew cheese money on crops and leather onesies. I packed a bag with dildos, paddles, and other instruments of torture. If I was going to be a domme, I was going to be a prepared domme.

Ophelia came with me the first time. On the outside, we looked like two average, thirty-something women in New York. Ophelia in her stylish, faux-leather coat. Me in an green wrap around, a giant purse, and an orange beanie.

No one on the subway would guess that I was wearing a full, Matrix-style, skin-tight bodysuit underneath, and my bag was packed to the brim with sex toys.

The C train rumbled into Manhattan, metal scraping metal, and my nerves began to bang around inside my body. My body got hot under the suit, which left no room for my skin to breath, and my mouth went dry. Ophelia kept trying to talk me through it, reminding me to establish boundaries and safe words and *don't forget to have fun.* I took my water flask out, sipping nervously, trying to distract myself from the growing imposture syndrome.

All I could think was:

He's going to clock you immediately for what you are. A fraud, a fake, a failure—

The train spat us out on the Lower East Side—once, Manhattan's creative community, full of hipsters and artists. Like everything in Manhattan, it was now mostly commercial, but if you looked hard enough, you could still find bohemian remnants growing like flowers in-between slabs of concrete. We passed thrift stores, a Ramen restaurant, and followed Dorian's address to an apartment building wedged side-by-side with a bookstore called "The Paper Cut."

Dorian's apartment building was marked with a red door. I found his name on the doorbell and buzzed him, lifting up to look in the fisheye camera.

Dorian's voice crackled through: "Be right down."

The front door buzzed, unlocking, and Ophelia and I went in. We entered a small lobby with an elevator and a winding set of stairs. The elevator lowered, revealing Dorian behind a set of iron teeth.

I'd remembered him being attractive when we'd met, but I'd hoped it was some sort of fluke, a trick of the romantic lighting at Cure. But here we was, looking devastatingly handsome. Dorian wore dark, creaseless slacks. A relaxed t-shirt. I took in those intelligent, blue eyes. The smooth, short beard that outlined the sharpness of his jaw. Dark hair that swooped across the top of his head and hung around his ears.

And there was that phenomenon—with Ophelia there, I wasn't only seeing him through my eyes, but through hers, too. I trusted her judgment more than anyone, so I knew he was *hot*, hot when even she took in a small, tight inhale.

He looked at us, frowned—that displeased, grumpy scowl —and I thought: *Ah, there he is. My favorite asshole.*

"Dove," he said.

"Dorian."

His eyes clocked Ophelia. "Who is this?"

"Your worst nightmare." Ophelia clicked her tongue against her teeth. "You gonna let us in or what?"

He stepped back, dramatically extending an arm to motion us into the elevator.

We stepped inside. He closed us in—which felt a bit like being locked in a cage. The elevator rose and we stood side by side—Dorian on one side of me, Ophelia on the other. I stared ahead, trying to match Ophelia's don't-fuck-with-me energy, but every now and then, I could feel Dorian watching me.

The elevator stopped and Dorian pulled back the gate. It entered right into his house, opening to a lamp-lit studio apartment with wooden floors.

Ophelia brushed passed him, her shoulder knocking against his. "I'm going to look around," she said. "Are you cool with that?"

He motioned around. "Help yourself."

I followed in behind her and stood there, arms crossed. My gaze skipped around the apartment, trying to ignore the imposture syndrome that kicked like a rabbit in my chest. It was a strangely tidy, clean apartment— except for the books. He had books stuffed in his bookshelf, books piled up in corners, books stacked on books on books.

Even as Ophelia went through his apartment, moving

from room to room, I felt his eyes remain hooked on me. He watched me, waiting for me to make the first move.

Finally, he asked, "Can I get you anything?"

"I'm good."

He squinted. "Are you sure?" The look in his eyes said: *I know you're not.*

Right—I was supposed to tell him to do things.

"You can fetch me some water."

He did. He poured a glass of water and came back with it. I took the glass and took slow, cold sips.

Ophelia returned. "What the fuck is this?" she asked Dorian. She had a gun in her hand and she waved it in his face. "Planning on kidnapping and killing her, huh?"

Dorian opened his palm. "May I?"

Ophelia handed over the gun. He took it from her and, without hesitation, put it to the side of his head and pulled the trigger.

I flinched. A tiny, yellow foam ball popped out of the gun, bounced off his forehead, and rolled to the floor.

"It's a Christmas gift," he explained. "For my nieces."

Ophelia clicked her tongue. "Likely story." She opened her palm. "ID."

He went to his coat on the coat rack, pulled out his wallet, and handed his ID. Ophelia snapped a picture of it with her phone, then handed it back.

"If you hurt her," she said, "I won't take this to the police. I'll just come over and kill you myself."

"Noted."

She turned to me. "You good?"

I nodded.

"The stage is yours." She followed Dorian with her eyes as she left. "Don't do anything I wouldn't."

She re-entered the elevator, closed the apartment door behind her, and clicked the button.

"You have to pull the gate," Dorian said.

She yanked it. It unfurled, then caught.

"You have to yank it," Dorian added unhelpfully. "Hard."

She pulled until it clicked into place. The elevator finally kicked into gear, humming. As it lowered her, her face vanishing in the small circular window, Ophelia flipped Dorian a parting bird.

Now, we were alone. In his apartment.

"I like her," Dorian said.

I couldn't tell if he was being sarcastic or not, so I held out the glass of water.

"I'm done with this," I told him.

He took the glass and set the water next to the toy gun down on the kitchen table. Hands now free, I took off my beanie. Then I unknotted my belt and dropped my coat, letting the heavy material fall to the floor.

It was worth it for the way Dorian's eyes got wide as he took me in. Skin tight, black latex hugged every inch of me, leaving very little to the imagination. For a second, I was pleased with myself. I'd shocked him speechless.

"So," he said.

I narrowed my eyes at him. "Did I say you could talk?"

"No."

"Yet you're doing it again. Disrespectful boy." I pushed passed him. I began to take a slow stroll around his apartment. I was trying to give off *badass vibes*, but the truth was, my nerves were rattling around inside of me and I needed to walk them off.

Out of the edge of my vision, I saw Dorian follow me. He took a seat in the living room on his emerald green, plush couch.

I sized up his space. "Look at this apartment. Full of... stuff." I lifted a worn, thick book from his shelf. "What even is this?"

No response from him. I turned to face him.

"Hello? Can you hear me?"

He tilted his head. "Can I talk? Can I not talk? I'm confused."

I pressed my lips together. "You can talk when I ask you a question."

He nodded to the book in my hand. "That's a first edition of *Frankenstein*."

"You have a thing for mad scientists?"

"I have a thing for monsters."

I continued scanning his apartment. Looking for reasons to hate him, and finding none. Hyper aware of his eyes, watching me. Waiting for *me* to make a move.

I spun around, facing him. "Have you been a good boy?"

"How do you mean?"

"Last time we spoke, I gave you a task. Do you remember it?"

He nodded slowly. "You told me not to jerk off until we met again."

"And? Did you succeed?"

"Oh, no."

The blasé, fuck-you way he said it made my eyebrows hike up my forehead. Shocked, but not surprised. Submissive boys were just like every other boys: entitled, fucking pricks. Anger washed through my veins, hot as lightning.

"*No?* It was a pretty simple fucking task."

He simply lifted a shoulder in a shrug.

Maybe Ophelia *should* come back. I was going to murder him.

I squared off in front of him. "When?"

"When what?"

"When did you jerk off?"

Thinking: maybe he broke on day five. Day six? Maybe seven days was too much…

"As soon as I got home," he said. "I thought about the way you arched your back when I rubbed your foot. The little moans you made when I pressed into your arch. I came so hard, I pulled a muscle."

Well, okay, that image was hot, but—"You didn't even try."

The look in his eyes…oh, he was enjoying this. He enjoyed being a little disobedient brat. "Was that a question?"

"Shut up." I closed the space between us and grabbed him by the throat. My grip forced his chin up, so those sharp eyes met mine. "You're lack of self-control is fucking pathetic. Do you know that?"

I could feel him breathing hard against my thumb. "Yes."

"What are you going to do about it?"

He struggled. Said nothing.

I tightened my grip.

"That was a question."

"Punish me," he sputtered.

"What?"

His voice came out in a hungry rasp. "Punish. Me."

That was what I promised—wasn't it? If he disobeyed, I would punish him.

The only problem was: I didn't actually think this all the way through.

Because, honestly, it didn't even cross my mind that he would disobey. No—*gleefully* disobey. I'd always been an obedient submissive. My Doms said *jump* and I'd ask *off what?*

Dorian was a different breed entirely. Now I'd made a promise, and I had to follow through on it. I had to teach him a lesson.

I paced over to my purse. I unzipped it and began going through it. I grabbed the meanest looking item I could find—a leather flogger with heavy strips hanging from it.

I closed the distance between us, toy in hand.

"Do you know what this is?"

His eyes flickered over it. "A flogger."

"Yes. And do you know what I'm going to do with it?"

His eyebrows knitted. "Do *you*?"

I slapped him. Hard. Across the cheek.

I didn't think about it. I'd never slapped a man in my fucking life. Even the ones who probably deserved it. No—definitely deserved it. But now here he was now, blinking at me, his face sunny and red.

Immediately, shame washed through me.

"I'm sorry," I stammered out. "Did that hurt?"

"Yes. It did." Smooth as a cat, he shifted off the couch. He fell to his knees on the carpet in front of me. He turned his head, giving me his other cheek. "Do it again."

But now my heart was pounding. *Pounding.*

I did a bad thing. I reacted out of *anger*, not out of play.

All I could think was: I'm a bad domme. I'm a terrible domme. I'm the worst thing a dominant can be. I'm a *dim-domme.*

Ignorant. Inexperienced. Reactive. Out of her depths.

Fuck. *Fuck.*

He remained kneeling, silently waiting for me to make the next move. Guilt rose like vomit in my throat. I found myself pacing the room.

"Are you okay?" I could barely hear Dorian's voice through the thudding of my own heartbeat.

"Fine," I lied. I went to the window, pushing open a curtain, and stared out. A couple stories down, someone was walking their dog. A little girl was holding hands with her mother. I tugged at the collar of my outfit. The wet-suit style material was clinging to my throat in a way that made it hard to breath. The zipper was in the back and I reached behind, trying to tug it open just a crack, but it wouldn't budge. The zipper was stuck in the cheap material, locking me in.

I could hear Dorian get to his feet. "Do you need something? Water?"

"I need…" The world tilted, spun. I felt myself sway on my feet and I gripped his bookcase, bracing myself and closing my eyes. I felt suffocated, like the whole outfit was one big boa constrictor, gluing my sweat to me.

"Scissors," I said.

"…Scissors?"

"Scissors," I choked out. I gripped at the suit. "I need you to cut me out of this. Immediately."

"Hold on." I could hear Dorian's quick footsteps. I shut my eyes closed, my heart roaring in my ears, and tried to do what he said. Tried to *hold on*. But my head felt light as I took in quick, shallow sips of breath. Was this a heart attack? Was I going to die in this latex prison?

Suddenly, Dorian's hand touched the back of my neck. "Don't move," he said, and I stopped squirming. His voice was calm, low, and I leaned into it. The blade felt cool against my skin. The scissors hissed, the blade sawing through the cheap fabric, and with every cut, I felt myself coming free. Like a butterfly busting out of a too-tight cocoon, wings trapped and damaged. He used the blade to cut along the zipper line and I felt the cold touch of the sharp metal slide across my back, down my spine. I forced myself to stay still, even as my body trembled.

When he finally had sliced through enough to free me, I untangled myself from the suit, shedding it from my arms, torso, and legs like snake skin, until I was down to nothing but my panties. But pride was pretty low on my priority list. *Breathing.* That was the thing. I lowered myself onto my hands and knees. I could feel the carpet underneath my palms. Every stitch of fabric pressing into my skin.

"Hey." Dorian's voice. I glanced up and saw him on his

hands and knees too, on my level. Those blue eyes hooked me in. "Look at me. Breathe. Can you do that?"

I sucked in a breath. Exhaled. "Good," he said. "Again."

I did. With each breath, I could feel the rapid flutter of my heart slowing. I felt like I had been very far away from my body, but Dorian was here, reeling me in, like a kite that had gotten swept too far in a gust of wind.

"You're okay," he said. "You're doing great."

My voice returned. "Sorry," I croaked out. "Sorry. I don't know what happened."

"I think you had a panic attack."

"Oh."

Those eyes met mine. "Tell me what you're feeling."

I swallowed. "I tricked you. I'm…I'm not a domme. I mean, I know what kink is, I used to be a submissive but…I don't know what I'm doing. I just…I thought I'd try it out. You know? I went through…a really fucked up break up. I wanted to reclaim my power or whatever. But now I'm just…naked on your floor, trembling. So." Self-pitying tears stung the back of my eyes. I sniffed, trying to hold them back. "Now I just feel stupid."

His lips pressed into a tight line. "Do you know what top drop is?"

I shook my head. "Not really."

"What about sub drop?"

"Sort of."

"Okay. So think of it like…the moment when, inexplicably, there's a switch. The submissive asks for pain. The dominant provides the pain. But then, against logic, against knowing that the submissive has consented to this, the dominant still feels…guilt. Like they've done something wrong. They might hate themselves for it. Feel ashamed." He paused for a moment. "You're not a bad domme. Or a bad person. You're just human. It's your brain, lying to you."

I looked at him. "I was so mean to you."

"Yes."

"I slapped you."

"I requested it. Remember?"

"Why?"

"Why what?"

"Why do you want me to hurt you?"

He hesitated at that. "Because I like it. It feels good for me. And I know you don't mean it. You're not a cruel person, Dove. You're a good girl."

I snorted out a laugh. How ironic—I finally got a guy to call me a *good girl*, but he was a masochistic submissive.

"You really are into this, aren't you?" I asked.

"Yes," he said plainly. "I really am into this." He paused, and then seemed to come to a decision: "I'll get you some clothes. Let's sit down. Decompress for a minute. When you're ready, I'll get you a cab home."

I thought about it. He was giving me an out. I could walk away and forget all about this humiliating evening.

But then I looked at him. I had this handsome, well-spoken, confident man on his knees. There was something disarmingly open about him—the clarity of his want, his frank honesty with me, and the complete lack of judgement from him—that drew me in.

I sucked in my bottom lip. I made my decision. "Show me."

"Sorry?" he asked.

"I want to try again. Show me what you're into."

* * *

I left the skinsuit carcass dead on Dorian's living room floor. He gave me a t-shirt with the book cover of *Dracula* on the front and a pair of sweatpants. Both were far too big on me and I had to make big, bunny ear loops out of the drawstring to keep it on my hips.

I went to the bathroom. I rinsed off my face. I pulled myself together. When I came back to the living room, feeling much more like myself, Dorian was waiting for me. He gave me a soft smile.

"You know," he said, "I like this look much better."

I flipped him the bird. "Smart asses get bruised asses."

A surprised laugh left him. *Oh.* I like that sound.

"Believe it or not, I'm being entirely serious." He motioned to his bedroom, then said, "After you."

I stepped into his bedroom. It was masculine—dark and wooden tones, bare brick on the back wall, the curtains drawn. A bachelor vampire cave. He moved passed me—the solid form of his body briefly brushing mine—and moved to a large, wooden chest at the foot of his bed.

I leaned against the doorframe and crossed my arms.

"Antique chest. Dark room. I feel like I'm about to play with submissive Nosferatu."

Half bent, Dorian looked up at me and lifted his eyebrows. "Respect the chest," he chastised.

Then he lifted the lid.

A spring-loaded compartment drew up, revealing an array of toys meticulously arranged and sorted on a bed of purple velvet. Things made of steel and glass, twisted into different shapes. My eyes fell to a couple things I recognized —arm restraints, a stainless steel dildo—and lingered on a few things I did not recognize—a particularly wicked looking device with different prongs and attachments sprouting from it like a painful bouquet.

I stepped over to the chest and walked my fingers thoughtfully over the edge of the drawer. I felt Dorian's gaze on me, measuring my reaction. "Quite the collection you've got here."

"It's not mine," Dorian said. "It's yours. See anything you like?"

My fingertips brushed a leather collar, and suddenly my chest went tight.

In a flash, I remembered—

* * *

The night of our fight. Being pinned down in my own bed. Shawn's large hands around my throat, layered over the black and pink collar. Choking, squeezing, popping the life out of me.

"This is what you wanted, isn't it? Say it."

No. No, I didn't like this. I loved pain—I loved his domination —but this...not like this.

Not with the anger in his voice.

Too afraid to tell him, I choked out, "Yes, master. Please. More."

* * *

I quickly retracted my fingers from the collar.

Dorian was still watching me, waiting patiently for me to make a decision.

I resettled myself. *You want this,* I reminded myself. *You're in control here. You control the scene.*

I hunted until I found what I wanted. A small, steel tool. It was a thin rod and, at the end of it, there was a small wheel with tiny, prickly metal spikes bursting from it. I picked it out from its small velvet container.

Dorian straightened his spine, moving in closer to me. "The Wartenberg Wheel," he said. "Good choice. Have you used one before?"

I was tempted to lie and tell him I had, but we were past the point of pretend so I said honestly, "I've seen them used but haven't actually played with one."

He held his palm to me. "Permission to demonstrate?"

I handed it over. "Granted."

He took my wrist in his hand and flipped it over so the soft underside of my arm was upward. Gently, he dragged the wheel across my skin. The pinpricks made me suck in a breath. They were sharp, but not enough to draw blood. Instead, they left a pleasant, stinging sensation up my arm.

"It's sharp," he said. "But you have to press in really hard to do damage."

He flipped it over in his hand and held out the handle of the wheel in offering.

"Do you want to try it?" he asked.

I nodded. I took the wheel, holding it between my fingers. Then I mimicked his motion, rolling the spikes from his wrist to the crook of his arm. He, likewise, pulled in a small gasp.

The sound of his hitched breath send a rush of heat through me.

Oh. Fuck. *Did I enjoy that?* I had to test this out.

I cocked my head thoughtfully. "Take off your shirt," I told him. "And sit on the bed."

He removed his shirt, revealing a strong chest underneath. A grove of soft, black hair that swept down his front and tapered like sand in an hourglass. He sat on the burgundy duvet and put his palms down on the mattress, exposing himself for me. I stood in front of him. I slowly dragged the wheel down his chest. It snagged on a couple of those fine hairs, which made him wince, but he didn't protest. I was taking my time with him now. I ran the spikes down the center of his body, admiring the small, red pinprick marks they made here. He groaned, a deep, wanting sound that vibrated through me. I pressed in harder as I reached his hips and he flinched, squirmed, and whimpered, but kept his hands obediently at his sides, letting me explore his limits.

That was when I realized: *I wanted to hurt this man.*

Like, really, actually hurt him.

What was it about him? His masculine entitlement? His pretty, disobedient blue eyes? The challenge hidden in his smirk? Or was it the way his lips parted and he moaned every time I hurt him like it was the most delicious kind of ecstasy?

Was it the fact that he wanted this, too?

I dragged it over his belt and hit the fabric of his slacks. I ran the wheel against the outline of his hard cock, tenting the material. "Wait," he said, and I stopped. Those sharp eyes met mine. "Just…this first time. Let's keep it above the belt. If that's okay."

Big eyes. Sweet eyes.

I told him, "That's okay by me, sweet boy."

He shuddered.

I grinned. "Do you like that? Do you like being my sweet boy?"

"Yes, mistress."

His eyelids were dropping. He was dipping into sub space, and, holy fuck…

I was enjoying this. Just as much as he was.

"Not mistress," I said.

He blinked, his vision briefly refocusing. "Sorry?"

"*Mistress.* I don't like the word. It makes me feel like I'm your dirty little secret."

"Understood. What would you like me to call you?"

I had to think about that one. I came up with: "Boss."

"Boss?"

"Yes. *Boss.* Should remind you of who is in charge. Plus, it makes me feel like I'm some… super villain and you're my naughty little henchman."

A small grin quirked over the corner of his mouth. "Yes, boss."

A thrill chased through me at that word on his tongue. I slipped my hand through his hair. I gripped it, feeling the soft curls protest under my tug. His head went back and he swallowed visibly as I raised the wheel. "Now," I said, "lay back and let me have fun with you."

6

A GIFT TO WOMEN EVERYWHERE

Dove. **Now.**

My phone pings with a notification.

> THE SEEKERS CLUB
>
> Happy birthday to Ophelia.
>
> She's such a good girl, she's invited everyone to her party tomorrow at nine. Click here to RSVP.

It's that time of year again.

I click the RSVP link and hit *I'm going.*

Every year, Ophelia throws a big birthday party. As she should. She's a queen and deserves to be celebrated. Plus, her birthday is close enough to Christmas that it doubles as a Christmas-birthday celebration.

It's always a great time, often involving too much booze and more than a couple regrettable mistakes. But her guest list is very specific. She invites only people in the Seekers' Club.

But I haven't gone back to the Seekers Club since I broke up with Shawn. Besides Ophelia, I haven't seen most of these people in nearly a year.

The last time they saw me, I was Shawn's pet.

Now when I see them, I'll be all alone.

And I'll do it. For Ophelia. I'll smile and have fun and make sure her birthday party is a goddamn blast, because she deserves it. But the truth is, the thought of seeing all those people again solo is soul-crushing.

Luckily, Cheese Louise is bustling.

It's called Cheese Louise because, one, the name is adorable, and two, the owner Marvin's wife is Louise. So it's a nice, romantic homage to the love of his life.

If my legacy was a store filled with cheese, I'd be pretty tickled pink about that.

I picked up this job on a whim but I've become something of a cheese expert in my short time working here, if I do say so myself. I spent my first few weeks sampling everything and staring at the assortment from behind the counter. But most of all, I love creating charcuterie boards. It's not unlike creating a painting—I can match colors. Put in some prosciutto to add a pop of pink among the beige and blues. I like finding tastes and textures that complement each other. I build the plates as though each cheese has its own personality and I'm creating a tiny, edible little family.

December is our busiest month. Everyone wants a nice charcuterie board for their holiday party. Packages of cheese wrapped up in pretty bows. Plus, Marvin has been in and out —he gets terrible colds in the winter—so I've been working like a dog to pick up the slack.

I lock up the cheese shop, smelling like brie with fingers bent and sore from pinching tiny bows, and—holy fucking shit.

There he is. *Dorian*. Out in the wild. Sitting at *our bar*—the wine bar where we first met in person across the street. He looks nice—in a dark button up, the sleeves rolled up to reveal those strong forearms. His beard groomed around the severe cut of his jaw, hair flopped to the side. He's at the window table—*our table*—the table where we first met face to face. He's sipping a glass of red wine, his eyes trained on a book in front of him. He's wearing reading glasses, which does strange things to the beat of my heart.

How much is that doggy in the window?

I should keep walking. Approaching him now would be breaking the unspoken lines we've drawn to protect our world from the real world.

But there is something about him that brings out the *bitch* in me.

I cross the street and enter Cure.

I'm met with dim lighting, dark walls, sexy vibes. The price tag is a little out of my range, but if I get off work early, I can usually make good on their happy hour before stumbling back to Brooklyn.

I unlatch the clasps of my jacket, peel it over my shoulders, and approach Dorian's table. He's so engrossed in his book, he doesn't even notice me until I've set my jacket over the chair and dropped my body in the seat across from him.

"Whatcha reading, pup?" I ask.

He looks up at me from under those dark commas of eyebrows. He blinks, as though he thinks I must be a mirage and he can shake me from his vision.

Not gonna lie, the hint of fear in this hard man's face is an aphrodisiac.

"What are you doing here?" he asks. His voice is tight.

"Good to see you too. Oooh. Are these olives?"

He's got a small bowl of green and black stuffed olives in the center of the table. He opens his palm, motioning for me to help myself.

I pop one in my mouth. An explosion of salty bitter bursts between my teeth.

"I'm starving. I just got off work. Didn't have a second to breathe."

His gaze slides out the window. He finds Cheese Louise and nods. "That's your shop?"

"The shop I work at, yeah. I don't like, own it. Which is good. If I did, I'd just eat all the cheese. All day every day." Another olive. "Hey, so what're you doing tomorrow night?"

He closes his book. The Moonstone by Wilkie Collins. The boy likes a gothic mystery—noted. "I imagine you're about to tell me."

He starts to pull off his glasses, but I tell him, "The glasses stay on." He pauses, readjusts them on his face. I lean back in my chair, admiring the view. "I'm going to a party. I want you to come."

"Why?"

"I haven't seen most of these people in, like, a year. I could just...use back up. Or whatever." Another olive. "God, these are addicting, huh?"

He stares at me like I've grown a second head.

"You want me to be your boyfriend for a night?"

The look in his eyes makes me want to run. I shake my head. "Forget it. It's a big ask—"

"When do I pick you up?"

"Sorry?"

"The party. If you want me there, I'll be there." He talks about this like a business deal, and my nerves settle, because this is *exactly* why I knew he'd be a good choice for this. He understands boundaries and compartmentalizing. One night out playing girlfriend/boyfriend won't kills us. Right? Those blue eyes meet mine. "When do I pick you up?"

"You can meet me at The Hideaway on Bleeker at nine."

"Okay. I'll be there."

I relax in my seat. *Problem solved.* For now, anyway. And maybe because I'm relaxing, that's when I notice…

There's a place setting in front of me.

I blink. "Are you on a date?"

He stares at mè. "Would you be jealous if I was?"

Dick. He just wants to get under my skin. I'm not allowed to be jealous about this. We negotiated this. We said dating was *okay.* So why this strange tingling in my chest?

I lean back. I examine him. "You're off to a shitty start."

A slow blink. "Excuse me?"

"No flowers? God. Men have gotten so lazy. Straighten up in your seat."

He's been hunching towards me. Now, he stiffens his spine. I draw my eyes over him and click my tongue disapprovingly.

"Black on black. What are you, a mortician?"

"It pays to be prepared."

I stifle a laugh. It comes out as a derisive snort instead. "Do you think you're funny?"

"On occasion."

"If you really want to make her laugh, you should take off your pants. Really give her something to giggle about."

He doesn't budge, but I see his breath pick up, chest rising and falling a little more rapidly. He loves it when I'm mean to him. And me?

I'm having way too much fun.

I lean forward. "Here's the plan," I tell him. "And you're going to listen to me. Word for word. Understand?"

"Yes, boss."

"Let her get whatever she wants. Don't let the waiter take your plate while she's still eating. Hold your plate until she's done. She's going to say she's too full for dessert but get her dessert anyway. Pay for her meal. Tip 25%. Minimum."

The candle flickers between us. His hand rests on the

table and I put mine next to his. Discreetly, I draw a single finger up and down the side of his pointer finger. Slowly. Barely touching him. The way I did with his cock earlier.

The muscles in his jaw tightens.

I take his wrist in my hand. I push his sleeve up, rolling it back. Exposing his forearm and the spidering veins underneath his skin.

"Are you going to read my palm?" Dorian asks.

I flatten my hand over my palm. "Let's see…is Dorian going to be a good boy tonight?"

I lift the tea candle from the table. I tilt it over his forearm. The flame flickers as liquid wax pools against the side of the glass.

My eyes connect with Dorian's. He's gone very still, but he's not safe wording.

He's bracing. Green light.

I tilt the candle a little more. The wax dribbles out and drips onto his forearm.

He jerks back instinctively, but I have my hand around his wrist, holding him into place. He sucks in a quick breath as the wax drips onto his skin, rolling in thick, white drops down his arm.

I watch him. He's watching the wax drip. Then those blue eyes lift to meet mine.

"Don't make her take the subway," I continue. "You buy her a cab. Take her home. What are you going to do if she wants to have sex?"

"I'm going to be a gentleman," he says. The low, hungry brass in his voice is like catnip to the dominant predator inside of me.

"A gentleman?" My voice pitches. "Women don't want a gentleman. They want a man who can make them come. Your body is mine. And you're going to use it to renew that woman's faith in men everywhere. You're going to give her the best night of her life.

"You're going to kiss her until she's weak in the knees. Touch her. Slowly. The back of her neck. Her thighs. Her face. I want her dripping wet before her panties even come off, understood?"

His eyes are dark. Unfocused. I let another sliver of wax fall and he winces as it splatters across the soft skin of his wrist. "Yes, boss."

"Then you're going to lick her cunt. You're going to feast until your jaw hurts and then you're going to keep going. Make her come on your tongue. Only after you've given her a nice, shuddery-leg orgasm, you're going to fuck her. You're not going to bang her like some college freshman rutting for his orgasm. Your orgasm is going to be the furthest thing from your mind. You're going to give it to her slowly. Let her feel every inch of that monster. Are you taking mental notes, pup?"

"Yes, boss."

"Good, because here's the important part. You're not going to come. Fake it if you have to. But your orgasms are mine. I know it's going to be a challenge when she's all whimpery and clenching around your cock. But good boys hold it in. You're a good boy, aren't you? Say it."

He's gone. So far gone. His eyes have that dumb, sub-space haze to them. "I'm a good boy."

I flick the wax with my thumb nail. It's dried and gone hard. It's turned white and looks pretty suggestive, frozen into pearly drips down his arm.

I put the tea candle down. I then lift his arm, guiding his hand to the side of my face.

My eyes meet Dorian's. His eyes suddenly widen, when my plan seems to register.

"Don't," he says, his voice tight.

Holding eye contact, I kiss his wrist. I slide my tongue over the wax over his arm. It tastes like a crayon, but I don't care. I'm addicted to the heat in his eyes, and I press my tongue flat against it, like I'm sucking it off.

"Fuck," Dorian hisses. He jolts—a small shudder, his body jerking forward—and by the sudden look of shame that crosses his face, I wouldn't be surprised if he just ruined his pants.

He glances down in his lap. "Fuck," he whispers.

Yep, definitely ruined his pants.

Cure is never going to let us back in here.

I grin. "Have a good night, champ."

I get up, pull on my coat, steal one last olive, and go to the exit. I pause to wrap my scarf around my neck against the bitter cold.

Just as I'm exiting, I nearly run into a woman who is entering. Dark-haired. Cute. I open the door for her and hold it.

"Oh! Thank you."

"You're welcome."

By which I mean: *you're so fucking welcome for the night you're about to have.*

I watch as she takes my seat, all bubbly smiles. Dorian rakes his hand through his thick curls, pulling himself together, and smiles politely back.

Before I leave, his eyes connect with mine through the window. Just a second more.

I give him a grin and a thumbs up. *Be a good boy.*

He's fighting on a smile. He turns back to his date. I tighten my scarf and head to the train.

7

———

OKAY. MY TURN

Dorian. **Now.**

I am, above all, a fucking degenerate.

I'm starkly reminded of this fact as I sit uncomfortably in a puddle of my own cum, in the middle of a nice restaurant, as my dominatrix exists and my dinner guest enters.

Lo and behold: Dorian, a man who should have never been let off his leash. Should not be allowed outside. Is not safe for public consumption.

(Put a muzzle on me. I'm begging you.)

Dove and her orange beanie vanish from my line of vision. She's replaced with a slender, tall, raven-haired woman who spots me and marches over.

Maggie hooks her purse on the chair and drops herself into the seat across from me. She keeps looking over her shoulder, her dark hair swishing back and forth.

"Who was that?" she asks.

"Who?"

"Who? My brother, the damn owl. *Who?* You know who."

Maggie is my younger sister, but she has a complete lack of classic younger sister energy. My brother, the eldest, is all self-control and responsibility. I'm the middle child, invisible, best neither seen nor heard.

Then there's Maggie. She should've been our devil-may-care, wild child, but instead, she became the family's emotional core. Trapped in an otherwise emotionally stunted family, she's our bleeding heart—the one who cares, perhaps too much, about everyone at all times. After carrying two children, now she's become even more of a surrogate mom to the rest of us.

It must be exhausting, but she carries the load well.

She stares at me now, waiting on a response, her sharp blue eyes mirroring my own.

I clear my throat. "She's a friend."

"A friend or a *friend?*" She wiggles her eyebrows.

I press my lips together. "Did you come here to interrogate me?"

"Yes, actually." She begins to pick at the olives between us—Dove made a dent in them, but the bowl seems never ending. "I'm leaving to go to our parents' house tonight. They're having us over for Christmas. Are you coming?"

"Now why would I do that when no one wants me there?"

"*I* want you there," she says pointedly. "Your nieces want you there."

I try to ignore that gnawing shame clawing at my throat. "Maybe next year."

I have a gift back tucked in beside my legs. I lift it and move it over to Maggie's side of the table. "This is for the girls," I tell her. "Don't let them play with it inside of the house."

But Maggie won't let up. "*Maybe next year.* That's what you said *that* last year. You and Mark need to bury the hatchet eventually."

"Tell him that."

"Dori." She reaches across the table. She takes my hand. Her thumb is soft over the back of my hand. "You can't keep punishing yourself for this."

I pull away from her gentle touch. I fix myself an olive instead and pop it in my mouth. "Besides. I couldn't come even if I wanted to. I've got plans."

"With who?"

I cock my head. "Now who's the owl?"

She narrows her eyes at me. "The woman? The woman who was just here? You're making that up. I don't believe you. What's her name?"

"Dove."

"Fake. This is all fake."

"I'll send you a postcard."

But I've forgotten: *Maggie is not Dove.* When I show Dove my teeth, she bites back. When I speak to Maggie with the same caustic tone, she bursts into tears. My bitter sense of humor just sounds *bitter* to her, and her bottom lip swells and starts to tremble. "You're a dick," she says. "An absolute dick. You know that? If I have to spend another Christmas knowing you're alone...holing up like a goddamn turtle in your goddamn *Dorian-shell*, I'm going to lose it...I'm really going to lose it..."

Well, now *I* feel like shit.

Reminder: my sister is sniffling across the table because she feels *bad* for me, sorry *for me*; meanwhile, I've got a chip on my shoulder and a cum stain drying on my thigh.

I need to be euthanized.

I relent. This time, I'm the one who reaches across and takes her hand. I give it a gentle squeeze. "I won't be alone. I promise."

I have a long, long list of crimes. But one thing I've never done: broken a promise to my sister.

That seems to quell her. She sniffles, but she's stopped crying. She takes her napkin and dabs it across her face. Her mascara is running down her cheeks. "What is wrong with your arm?"

Oh. Right. There are bits of dried wax still attached to my skin.

I push my sleeve down, covering my shame.

I counter with: "What's wrong with your face? You look like you gave an octopus a blow job."

She lets out a sound that is half a bark, half a laugh. "I'm going to go clean up."

She gives my hand one more squeeze and then detaches from me. Maggie gets up and leaves the table. While she's gone, I pull out my phone. I text Dove:

ME

See you tomorrow, Boss.

8

—————

BOYFRIEND REPAIR

Dove. Now.

The mattress shifts as Ophelia rolls to her stomach, perched up on her forearms. Her beautiful, kinky curls bounce when she adjusts. "Is he seriously coming?"

I shrug. "I don't know. I give it a 50/50."

"I hope he does. I wanna hang out with the man you've got wrapped around your..."

"Whip?"

"Nah. Your whip wrapped around *his*..." She whistles, swirls a single finger in the air.

We cackle with laughter. We've both wonderfully, stupidly wine drunk. I roll over, belly crawl to the other side of the mattress, and pick up the bottle of wine, topping us both off.

"I am a gift to women everywhere," I tell Ophelia as we lay side by side in her bed. "People should pay me. Like a service, you know? Give me $300 bucks. I will train your boyfriend to be a better boyfriend. I call it...Boyfriend Repair."

"You break it, you buy it."

"I mean, sometimes you've gotta take things apart to put them back together...you know?"

"You're not wrong."

I take a thoughtful sip of wine. "Mm. Speaking of breaking things." Her bedframe is old school—rounded bars on both the head and foot of the bed. I prop up on her footboard, bend my knees, and knock my leg against hers. "Is Phantom coming to the party?"

"I think so."

"Is that going to be weird? If Brody proposes..."

A frown deepens on her mouth. "If Brody proposes, he'll be happy for me. Look—what I have with Phantom, it's great. But it only exists at the club. Brody...he takes me out on dates. He asks me how my day is. He cares about me. We have a chance at something real. It's time. You know?"

I *do know.* I get it. I think about that guy from the bar. *Thirty-five,* he said. *Good for you.*

Time slips, running away from you before you're ready. Everyone around me is trying to settle down, find love, build lives. What am I doing?

I'm going through second puberty, playing pretend as a dominatrix, *finding myself*, whatever the fuck that means.

As if she can sense the mood shift (because of course she can, she always knows what I'm thinking), Ophelia leans forward, extending her wine glass towards me. "Hey," she says, her dark eyes meeting mine, her voice dropping conspiratorially. "Whatever happens...let's fuck it all up. If this is my last night as an un-engaged woman, I want to go out in style. I want a blow-out, banged up birthday. I want to wake up the next day with bruises and not have any idea how they got there."

My grin returns. "To fucking up."
We clink glasses and drink ourselves to sleep.

9

YOU'RE A FUCK UP, CHARLIE BROWN

D̲ORIAN̲. Now.

This is a terrible idea. I should know. I'm an expert in terrible, no-good, self-destructive ideas. And yet, here I am.

Getting up to no good.

I should be at work, doing end-of-year accounting and inventory, wrapping and sending last-minute Christmas gift packages.

Instead, I'm freezing outside a bar called The Hideaway, waiting for the woman who pushes me on my knees and shoves her fingers in my mouth.

Mom, I hope you're proud.

Despite my black fleece coat, I'm freezing. Conveniently, I live just down the street. Unfortunately, that means I'm early, and I'm not going to head inside without Dove. I shove my hands in my pockets in attempt to revive the feeling in my fingers.

This is insane. She probably won't even show. Maybe she's testing you. Sending you on some wild goose chase just to see how devoted you are. Just to make you wait in the snow for hours. And like an idiot, like the absolute simp you are, you will, you'll wait here all night just to please her, just like you did with *you-know-who*, you never learn from your mistakes, you pathetic piece of—

The subway rattles underground. It coughs up steam through the grates which crystalizes into white smoke. From the bowels of New York City, Dove climbs the subway steps and the smoke clears for her.

Waves of auburn hair spill down and touch her shoulders. She's clutching a green, thick duffle coat. Her head tilts and I get a vision of her profile, haloed by the subway lights—a small, flat nose, thick lips that I constantly crave all resting on a sweet, round face.

Then her eyes find me—a deep emerald that matches the green glow of the twin orb lanterns heralding the subway exit, as though the very spirit of New York City lives inside of her, some restless and carnivorous demon. The instant her gaze settles on me, a smile crosses those perfect, kissable lips.

My heart punches through my chest, and any reticence I had about coming vanishes like so much city steam.

I'd do anything for this woman. Crawl across hot coal. Lick the snow from her boots. Let Santa sit on *my* lap—

"You came," she says.

"You're surprised."

"Well, yeah. It's kind of a crazy ask."

"I honor my commitments. Even the crazy ones."

She side-eyes me. "Especially the crazy ones?"

"Perhaps."

"Thank you," she says.

She sounds so genuine, so truly relieved that she doesn't have to go through this night alone, that I want to tell her that I would've done anything to be here, but instead what comes out is a terse: "Don't mention it."

Long ago, I enclosed my emotions inside a block of ice in my chest, and it's going to take more than her sweet eyes to thaw it.

"Are you going to tell me I look good?"

"Did you skin a Muppet to get that jacket?"

"Oscar the Grouch is chained to my radiator as we speak."

"Kinky."

"I'm got a type. Grumpy, filthy boys."

Her eyes fall to the item in my hand. I'd forgotten I was holding it. I hold it out to her. A bunch of roses.

"A wise woman once told me to always bring flowers to a first date."

She takes the flowers. She pulls them close and, with those green eyes on mine, she inhales in deeply.

Why is the sight of her smelling my roses so erotic?

"Roses," she says, her voice slow, as though she's measuring the weight of the word on her tongue. "Predictable." With a violent swing of her arm, she throws the whole thing in the metal trash bin. "Try harder."

Her gaze doesn't leave me the whole time. I can't please her, and I love it. My heart thumps wildly in my chest.

Is it wrong to meet your dominatrix's friends with half an erection? We're about to find out. We get inside and we're met with a burst of hot air. A blush hits her cheeks from the heat and she unfastens her coat, pulling it from her shoulders. Gently, I take it from her, draping it over my arm. She's wearing a red dress underneath that hugs her curves in all the right ways.

"Oh," she says, and she puts her hand on my chest when she says it. The second she touches me, my brain short circuits like the dumb animal I am, and I'm unable to comprehend the next words, which sound something like...

"Bytheway, allmyfriendsareSeekers."

"Your friends are...what?"

"Come on, let me introduce them."

She fists her fingers in my shirt and tugs, pulling me forward. I am at least a foot taller than her, but I let her lead me around like a horse with a bit.

It looks like Christmas exploded in The Hideaway. It's a dive bar, but cozy about it. The space is strewn with multi-colored Christmas lights and they're blasting rock and pop covers to holiday classics over the speakers. Many of the people in here are dressed in holiday "ugly" sweaters or Santa hats, and I clearly missed the memo, because I'm wearing my black coat, dark slacks, and a crisp grey shirt.

Dove drags us to the back, where there's a small group crowded around a table. Everyone is drinking out of festive Christmas mugs. They glance up when we arrive, and a jock of a man who looks like he could double as a pro-football player immediately stands up, slaps his hand on the table, and shouts: "Slap my ass and call me Scrooge, it's the ghost of Christmas past!"

Dove lifts her hand in a princess wave. By the way her friends are acting, I get the impression it's a pretty big deal that she came out tonight. They hoot and hug her like they haven't seen her in months—and I guess they haven't.

What did she say? It'd been close to a year?

I haven't seen shy-Dove in a long time. It's almost cute—the downturned eyes, the uneasy smile.

"Okay," she says, squeaking through a particularly bone-crushing hug. "Relax, guys. I didn't *die*, just…took a sabbatical. *And.* Look what I brought." She slaps her hand amicably over my shoulder. It's a dad move, and I almost expect her to introduce me as *champ*. "This," she announces, "is Dorian. Everyone say *hi, Dorian.*"

There's a round of uneven *hi, Dorians* spilling from the crowd. But when I really take in the group, that's when my blood goes cold.

Because I *recognize* some of them from the Club. Specifically: Phantom and Princess. The stoic Dom and the leggy blonde side-eye me from the corner.

My heart hiccups in my chest. *Please, don't use my old scene name. Please, give me anonymity for this one night. Please, please, please—*

"Dorian." Phantom nods slowly. "Nice to meet you."

Princess—as always—takes Phantom's cues. She cocks her head, her pigtails wagging like floppy dog ears, and flashes me a bright smile. "Cool!"

I exhale. My secret is safe. For now, anyway.

"Thank you for letting me crash your party," I say.

Ophelia flicks her hand. "People are always like, hey, Ophelia, why do you have your party so close to Christmas? And the thing is, most of us don't have anywhere else to be for the holidays. So. Welcome to the island of misfit toys."

A problem I know too well. I've been ostracized from my family (well, everyone except Maggie) for my deviant behavior. I imagine many at this table have, too. That's a thought that'll make my throat too tight if I linger on it, so I change the subject. "Sounds like I'm in good company." I reach into my coat, where there's a large pocket in the inner lining. I pull out a small, wrapped present and hand it over. "Just a little something. Happy birthday."

She blinks at the gift, genuine surprise crossing her features. "Aw. You shouldn't have." But she rips into the present anyway. When the Santa wrapping paper peals back enough to reveal the gift underneath, she breaks out in large, cackling bouts of laughter.

"Oh my God!" she shouts. "*Knot My Alien Mate!* I love this book! My copy went missing..."

Dove and I exchange a knowing glance.

* * *

Dove has this game she's affectionately titled: *Read and Weep*.

It goes like this: Dove straddles me while I lay on my back on my silk sheets in my bed. As often is the case, I am completely naked while Dove is still mostly clothed—she's in a bra and oversized sweater. She's wearing these cute, white panties with daisies on them and I catch a glimpse now and then, wrapped snugly around the curve of her lovely hips.

She's given me the book *Knot My Alien Mate*. It's a raunchy sci-fi novel about a woman who gets abducted by a blue-skinned, split-tongue, eight-foot alien. Naturally, they spend their whole time fucking on his jungle, alien planet.

My task is to read the book out loud to her. While I read, Dove sits on my thighs and slowly, tenderly, traces a long, soft feather over my naked skin. If at any point I stammer or stumble over a word, I have to restart the chapter.

If it doesn't sound challenging, you should know that after about fifteen minutes of this soft feather caressing the side of my neck, tickling the dip of my hips, and teasing the most sensitive spots of my swollen, leaking cock, I can barely think straight, let alone read a single sentence without moaning.

So far, we've read *chapter four* about twenty times.

I read out loud: "She sank down on his enormous manhood. She felt herself stretch around him and the hardened ridges on him sent chills of pleasure through her. Her thighs quaked as she slowly accepted his foreign girth, inch by inch, and...and..."

"*And?*" Dove repeats. She grips my hip, digs those sharp, kitten nails in.

The warring sensations—the burst of pain at my hip mixed with the too-light strokes of the tip of her feather grazing my erection—makes my cock jerk. I groan. I sweat. I try to refocus on the story, but I can barely see the words on the page.

I try to buy time: "I have a question about knotting," I say.

"Go ahead."

"So the…alien…his uh…*knot*…stays swollen the entire time he's inside of her?"

"Mmhm." The flick, flick of her feather makes me shiver.

I pant. I writhe. "What if…what if the alien needs a break?"

"The alien doesn't get a break." She presses a single, solid kiss to my chest, right where my heart is. It anchors me and I close my eyes for a brief, lovely moment of reprieve. She must feel my heartbeat pounding against her lips. She shifts, straddling one of my thighs, and even though the fabric of her panties I can feel the heat of her. The thought of slipping her panties aside and ending my torment by sinking myself into her tight, sweet heat is more than I can bear. My body flexes, drips, and I'm making a mess of us, my abdomen wet and stained. She drops the feather—now ruined and sticky— and picks up a brand-new feather. "The alien," she says, "should keep reading. You're getting to my favorite part."

She traces it up my thigh and the new softness is like fire on my skin. I grip the book as my eyes roll into the back of my head.

* * *

We're not coy. Ophelia catches our exchanged looks and squints at us. "But you wouldn't know anything about that, would you?"

"Nope," Dove lies.

"Not a thing." I follow suit.

"Mmhm." She flips the copy over to admire the painted edges. "This is a special edition, too. How the hell did you get a hold of this?"

"The perks of owning a bookstore."

Dove knits her eyebrows. "You own a bookstore?"

"I do."

She looks at me like I've just taken off my skin-suit in front of her and revealed a lizard head underneath.

"Okay," Ophelia says. "You *have* to see this." Then she takes out her phone, scrolls through it, and hands it over to me. "This was the gang last year. We *are* recreating this photo, by the way, so everyone get ready. Do not fuck this up for me!"

On her screen is last year's group photo. I stare at it. There are a few of the same people in this photo—Ophelia, Dove, Phantom, Princess. But Dove doesn't look like herself at all. It takes me a couple seconds to even pick her out from the crowd. Her hair is a shocking, bright blonde. She's dressed in a cute, pink baby doll outfit.

A man stands behind her. He's a ginger wearing a Christmas sweater and a grin that says he's a lucky bastard and he knows it. He has the hollow of her throat cradled in the palm of his hand. He holds her to him possessively.

I hate him. I hate every single one of his perfectly white teeth.

No. Be nice. Play nice. What would my therapist say? *Anger is your favorite masking response. Try something positive. Rephrase your negativity into something positive.*

I hope all of his dreams come true.

Specifically, the dreams where his teeth fall out of his mouth or where he shows up at work humiliatingly naked.

"Cute," I say.

Dove is smiling, but her face turns red.

Phantom lifts his beer and waves a finger between the two of us. "Are you her new Dom?"

Dove clasps her hand over the back of my neck. "No. I'm his."

Carver's eyebrows lift. "Dove. I didn't know you had a switch in you."

"Neither did I." Her hand tightens on my neck and she grins at me. "Turns out, I just needed to meet the right, pathetic puppy."

My heart does a strange skip in my chest when she claims me in front of her friends.

"On that note," I say. "Can I get anyone a drink?"

Her friends shake their heads, but Dove puts her hand on my arm. "I'll come with you."

We slip through the crowd of sweater-clad people to get to the bar. I flag down the bartender and put in our drink orders.

"Cabernet," I order for myself, "and a Jack and Coke for the lady. Did I get that right?"

She blinks at me. "Shockingly, yes."

"You talk. A lot. During our sessions. I've picked up a thing or two."

She laughs. "I didn't think you were listening."

"I know everything about you—how you take your cocktails. I know your favorite type of hat is *beanie.* I know that you wear your socks with clocks on them on days when you need a little pick-me-up because they make you feel like Maurice from Beauty and the Beast."

"Who doesn't want to be Maurice?"

"Everyone. Everyone doesn't want to be Maurice. Most women want to be Belle."

She shrugs. "The whole town thinks you're crazy and leaves you alone to tinker with toys all day? Sign me up for that."

I lean my elbows onto the bar, take out my phone, and crook my finger in Dove's direction. "Come here a moment."

She shifts in closer. I adjust my phone so we can see ourselves in the camera's eye. Even I have to admit—we make a handsome pair. She rests her chin on my shoulder. "Say *please.*"

"Please."

I snap the picture. Then I pull my phone back and drop the photo in a text.

"Who are you sending that to?" Dove asks.

"My sister. You met her. If I don't prove to her I'm being social, she'll send the battalion."

Sure enough, Maggie responds to my picture with a flurry of emojis—heart-eyes, heart-eyes, heart-eyes.

Dove cocks her head. "Your sister? When did I meet your sister?"

"At Cure. When you ate all my olives."

"*That* was your sister? So not a girlfriend?"

"No. Not a girlfriend. I'm all yours."

She's trying not to look pleased by that. She's failing. She shrugs a shoulder and leans against the bar. "Good. We still have so much training to do before I can set you into the wild."

"Like what?"

"Like..." She stares off across the bar, lapsing into thought. "We need to work on your emotional literacy."

"I'm listening."

"We've been playing for...what? Four months?"

"And two weeks."

"—And there's so much I don't know about you."

Oh. No. I feel my shoulders get tense. "You know plenty about me."

She makes a sweeping motion with her hand. "I know your hard limits and soft limits. I know what you like in bed. But I don't know anything about *you.* Dorian. The man."

It's by design, I want to tell her. I horde my secrets the way a dragon hordes gold.

The bartender slides over our drinks, finally. She takes a

slow sip from hers. She's staring at me, thoughtfully. "Tell me something about you," she says.

I think about it. "I finished *Knot My Alien Mate*."

She blinks. "You did? Without me?"

"I did. Without you. And the subsequent six sequels."

She laughs. "No fucking way."

"I had to. You left me on a cliffhanger."

There's that sly, Dove smirk. "Yeah, I guess I did, huh?"

She hand slips over my thigh, painfully reminding me of my own, aching cliffhanger, and I fight back an erection.

"Hey." The bartender (*go away, can't you see we're in the middle of something?*) appears in front of us and nods towards our group. "You guys with the birthday girl?"

Dove pulls away from me (*fuck you, bartender*). "Yeah, why?"

He reaches into his back pocket, pulls out a folded slip of paper, and hands it over to Dove. "Some guy dropped this off for her earlier today. Said to give it to her before you left."

"Thanks." Dove takes the paper and gives me a questioning look. "Mysterious..." she says, wiggling her fingers. She takes her drink and I follow her back to the corner table.

They've pulled up two extra seats. We only need one. I sit and Dove takes a spot perched in my lap. Her body fits perfectly in mine and I'm glad to have a drink in my hand. Otherwise, it'd be too tempting to slide my hand up her dress and...

"O," she says. She leans forward (the curve of her ass pressing into my hips) and extends the slip of paper towards Ophelia. "Check this out. I think Brody left it for you."

Ophelia takes the paper. She unravels it, and starts to read it in front of the group:

"*Dear Ophelia, I know how much you like a challenge. So tonight, Seeker, your present is a game of hide and seek. if you want me...you'll have to find me. I've left riddles inside Christmas ornaments in the key places across the city and*—oh, my God! A scavenger hunt! It's a scavenger hunt!" She lets out an excited, high-pitch squeal that momentarily silences the bar. She takes a deep breath. "Okay, okay…here's the first clue. It's a riddle. *You're so cold, yet you melt on my tongue.*"

Ophelia's mouth twists into a thoughtful frown. "So cold," she repeats. "And yet…"

Carver snaps. "Got it," he says. "It's a—"

"Snowflake!" Ophelia shouts. "Snowflake! I love this game!" She glances around at all of us. "What are you all doing sitting here? Go, go! Hunt for a snowflake!"

At her cue, we're off like race horses. Dove jumps off my lap with a force that momentarily winds me. Chairs scrape across the floor as everyone scatters around the bar to find the hidden ornament.

The bar is awash in shiny tinsel, dangling decorations, and a hodgepodge of multicolored lights. Every nook and cranny seems stuffed by something the owners picked up from the nearest Dollar Tree. The Hideaway it turns out is, in fact, a good hiding spot.

Dove darts towards the bar. She starts looking underneath the bar top to see if anything's been taped underneath, I image. She fondles the empty stools.

Clever girl.

She twists around and narrows her eyes at me. "Are you following me?"

"I'm afraid if we split up, one of us might die."

Dove turns to hide it, but a smile creeps up her lips.

Her hard-earned smiles are, by far, my favorite.

"Just so you know," she warns me, "Ophelia is, like, highly competitive." She ducks underneath another stool, causing the patron next to her to give her a peculiar glare. "So you're not far off. If you find the snowflake first, she might actually beat you to death with her shoe."

I lace my fingers together behind my back. "So I shouldn't mention the giant snowflake on the top shelf?"

Dove whips her head towards the bar. I watch as her eyes fall on it—there, top shelf, right in the center, are a pair of skis crisscrossed together. Sitting in front of them, a large ornament about the size of my head, with a glittering snowflake in the center of it.

"Dorian!" She smacks my chest playfully. I've unlocked a new kink: the light in Dove's eyes when she's won a game. "How did you find that so quickly?"

"I played a lot of I Spy growing up…I was a very lonely child."

She leaves her hand planted on my chest. "Lonely child-hood. Bookstore owner. Meddling sister. That's three things you've shared today." Her lips ghost over mine and the next two words come out in a sultry purr: "Good boy."

I've died. Gone straight to heaven.

Dove skips away from me. "Ophelia! We found it!"

She gathers the gang and everyone heads to the bar. We look like a motley mob ready to storm the barricades.

The bartender comes back around. He's got that amused look of someone who is in on the game, but playing it cool. "Can I help you?"

Ophelia points to the ornament. "We need that!"

"Ah. Yeah." He folds his arms. "You can have it. But it'll cost you."

Ophelia slams a palm on the table. "What kind of D&D fuckery is this? I have to roll a ten or some shit?"

"No," he explains. "But you do have to take a shot-ski."

He removes one of the skis from behind the bar. I can see now that the ski has a number of round divots in it. He fills them with shot glasses, and then fills the shot glasses with tequila. One for each of us.

"Oh," Princess says. "Not me. Sorry. I don't drink."

"No sweat." The bartender removes her shot and puts it in front of him instead. Then he winks at Ophelia. "For the birthday girl."

Ophelia has that wild, untamed energy that most find magnetic. I don't blame half the bar for flirting with her.

She's just not my type. My type is…well.

Standing right next to me, grimacing at the shot.

"Not a tequila fan?" I ask.

She puts on a brave face. "Not my drink. But we're in it now."

The bartender gives us a plate of salt and a lime wedges. I turn my hand into a fist and dust salt over the spiraled conch of my fingers.

"Lick," I tell Dove.

She slides her tongue over my thumb. I pull my hand to my mouth, cleaning off the remainder of salt. Then Ophelia counts to three and we lift the ski as a group. The height difference forces me into a half-bow, but I manage to knock back the shot. For the most part. It's a messier experience than I intended and some drips down my chin.

Dove gags. We lower the ski and I hold out a lime wedge for her.

"Suck."

Like a baby bird, she takes it from my hand. She sucks in the lime wedge, wincing and whimpering the whole way. When she lets go of it, I take her wedge and pop it into my mouth. The sour tang takes the edge off the tequila burn.

I feel Dove watching me. "Did you just take that from my mouth?"

"Mmhm."

She considers it. "I…learned something new about myself today."

I hum on a laugh. Spit out the lime and discard it in a pile of wilted rinds.

Ophelia reaches across the bar, grabbing air. "We did it! Now give me."

The bartender stretches up, plucks the ornament, and takes it down. He hands it over to Ophelia, who grabs it like a greedy squirrel with a particularly large nut.

"Okay, shut up, shut up, *everyone shut up!*" she shouts, even though we are all saying absolutely nothing. She twists the ornament and it pops open. There's a roll of paper inside. She unrolls it and spreads it across the bar, reading out loud:

Wind me up,
  Fit me through the eye,
  Send me your broken,
  And I'll return it revived.

Ophelia repeats the riddle, and the rest of us think on the words.

It's no Robert Frost, but I'll give Ophelia's boyfriend credit—it's creative.

Suddenly, Carver (the meathead, of all people) snaps his fingers. "Yo! It's a thread! Threads! The concert venue in Williamsburg!"

I feel my mouth form into a frown. "Brooklyn?"

Dove pats my back. "Saddle up, city kid. You're in for a long night."

1 0

———

JUDGE A BOOK BY ITS COVER

Dove. **Now.**

We walk to the train as a group. Ophelia leads the charge. She's already drunk, or flying high on the competitive adrenaline, or both, it's hard to say.

Good for her. It's her birthday, after all.

The second I'm outside, an arm swings around my shoulders. Carver locks me in a friendly hold and slows so we fall out of step with the rest of the group.

"Hey, stranger," he says.

I glance up at him. "Hey yourself."

The bright city lights cast shadows under his strong jaw. His gaze finds mine. "Last time I saw you," he says, "you were a slutty little submissive wearing pink collars and fuck-me heels."

I snort on a laugh. "Last time I saw *you*, you were a slutty playboy who hit on anything with a pulse. Some things change." I put my hand on my chest, gesturing to myself. "…

And some things do not." I give him a hard but amicable shove, putting some space between us.

He tucks his hands in his pockets as we walk. The ground is covered in snow salt and my boots crunch on it. "So this is you? Dove 2.0?"

"Same Dove. Just…slightly improved. Some of the kinks worked out."

"Not all the kinks, I hope." There's that Prince Charming, Carver grin. "I like him. By the way. Dorian. Big improvement over the last guy you were with. He was a dick."

"Yeah…"

Even the mention of Shawn feels like cracking grains of sand between my molars. I knew that was one of the dangers of coming here tonight. People were going to want to talk about it. Doesn't make it hurt any less. Luckily, Carver doesn't push it. Instead, he asks, "So what's the deal with the two of you?"

"How do you mean?"

Those green eyes hunt mine. "Are you exclusive?" He's walking close and our arms brush.

He's propositioning me. I realize: I haven't been propositioned to in a really, really long time. Not by anyone I would consider saying *yes* too, anyway.

It's been a year. I've healed. I've moved on from Shawn. I've even cut my teeth on dominating.

Could I do it again? Could I let someone dominant *me* again? Could I ever let myself be vulnerable like that again?

Carver *would* be a good test-drive Dom. I'm familiar with him. We've played before, and we're good at it. I like the heavy thud of his hand when he spanks. I like the way he grips my throat. I trust him to respond to safe words and respect my limits. More importantly, I trust him to stop if, halfway through, I decide I can't continue.

But even the thought of doing a scene with him makes my ovaries shrivel up inside of me.

The truth is: I don't *want* Carver.

I want…well.

I glance ahead. Dorian has paired up with Phantom. They're talking and I find myself entranced by Dorian. The quick step of his long legs. The way he shoves his hands in his pockets. The way that, every now and then, he turns his head back as though to make sure I'm still behind him.

I'm attracted to this guy for just existing. But I can't tell Carver that. I can't tell him that I want someone else—someone who will probably never want me *like that*.

But that's a problem for another day.

I shake my head. "I'm not playing with other people. Thank you, though."

He nods his head. It's a *no hard feelings* nod. "Cool. You know where to find me if you change your mind."

Dorian glances back at me again, but this time, he breaks away from his conversation. He stops and lets us catch up to him before walking in step with us. "What are we talking about?" Dorian asks.

He looks directly at Carver when he says it. He has a murderous look in his eyes. It's like he can *smell* Carver's pheromones.

"Shooting the shit," Carver grunts. The he holds up a hand. "Yo! Princess! Slow down a sec." Carver moves ahead, joining up with Princess instead. I can hear him say, "What the fuck've you got under those heels, jetpacks?

Dorian and I are on our own again. But he won't stop glaring at Carver's back.

"Hey. Look at me." Those blue eyes obediently snap to me. I grin. "Smile, baby girl."

Dorian attempts it. It looks like a Jack-o-Lantern grimace.

"Are you having fun?" I ask.

"Your friends are..."

"Kinky? Weird? Freaks?"

"My kind of people."

I can't explain the relief that floods my heart at the sound of that. I blink at him. "Really?"

"Yes."

Dorian slows our pace. I knock my shoulder affectionately against his and he lets me. "I've got to admit, Brody outdid himself on this one."

"Ophelia seems to be having a great time," Dorian agrees.

"She thinks he's going to propose," I tell him.

He side-eyes me. He narrates: "She says, like she just swallowed a bee."

"No, I mean...it's sweet. I guess. I just think big, flashy shows of affection are overrated. If you want to spend your life with me...tell me you want to spend your life with me. Don't make a big show about it."

A small grin touches Dorian's mouth. "No grand gestures for Dove. Noted."

We're near Dorian's apartment. We have to walk passed it to get to the subway. As we stroll past the adjoining bookstore, and one of the displays causes me to stop in my tracks.

I gasp. "Holy shit. It's the new Damaged Hearts book!"

The book has its own mini-display next to the words "New Release." The cover is made to look like it's been torn, revealing bits of text underneath. The standing book has a tag attached that reads: "Autographed Copy."

Dorian stands next to me. "A big Quinn Siobhan fan?"

I touch the glass between me and the book. "I love her. That series changed my life. I'm not exaggerating."

Dorian tilts his head. "You want me to get that book for you?"

"They're closed."

"For you, boss, anything." He picks up a brick and aims it at the window.

"Dorian! Red!"

He drops the brick. Then he reaches into his pocket, fishes out a key, fits it in the lock. He twists. The door pops open and he motions me inside.

Oh—wait. Duh. "This is your bookstore?" I ask.

"This is my bookstore," he confirms. "After you."

I walk inside. A small bell chimes above the door, announcing our presence. Immediately, I'm hit with my favorite smell in the world—printed paper, that stuffy, library smell. As Dorian goes to turn on the lights, I text Ophelia to let her know we've been detoured, and we'll meet them at Threads. She gives me a thumbs up.

I glance around. His bookstore reminds me of his apartment—a sort of rumbled charm to it, like the whole place just rolled out of bed. Shelves overstuffed. Postcards of vintage New York City scenes stacked haphazardly in a display. Antique lamps everywhere. A cat bed in the window. Tiny, folded index cards with *Staff Recommended* descriptions underneath favorited books.

"What is it about *Damaged Hearts*?" Dorian asks as he pulls a copy from the shelf.

I tickle my fingers over the spines of the local interest section. "I know what you're going to say. It's dumb smut."

He shakes his head. "I wasn't going to say that at all."

"It was my introduction to BDSM. I've got a soft spot for it. And I liked the characters."

"A man has an affair with his brother's wife. They're not incredibly likable characters."

I let out a faux gasp. "So you *are* familiar with the book!"

Dorian's lips thin. "You could say that."

I shrug. "I don't know. I liked Poe. I liked his unwavering, obsessive love. He knew it would ruin everything—his relationship with his family and his brother. But he did it. For Quinn."

He winces. "Be careful about the toxic men you romanticize."

"Why? Because I might end up in the back of a van?"

"Something like that."

"Look, Shawn was…Chernobyl level toxic. He made me feel like there was something wrong with me. Like I had to *earn* his affection. Poe was the complete opposite of that. I wanted the fantasy of a man who couldn't stand to be without me for a second, even if being *with* me was painful. Does any of that make sense?"

He goes quiet. There's a weight to our silence now.

Did I say something wrong?

"Stay here," he says. "I'm going to wrap your book, and then we can go meet up with your friends."

"Okay."

He leaves for the other room. I get up. I'm feeling bold— I've got a whole bookstore to myself. It's like being inside a museum after hours. A sacred space, now mine to explore.

I let myself wander. I know all bookstores have, basically, the same layout, but I'm getting a weird sense of déjà vu from this one. Like I've been here before. The whole bookstore is horror-themed. The horror section takes up the most space, spines of dark and red checkering the shelves.

"Do you only sell horror?" I call out.

Dorian's voice replies back from…somewhere deep in the shelves. "Mostly horror," he corrects. "I do sell other genres. Reluctantly."

I find a shelf labeled "Til Death do Us Part." Ah. This must be his romance section. My suspicions are confirmed by Dorian's choice in decoration. There's a copy of *Damaged Hearts* pinned to the shelf with a knife sticking out of the book.

I chuckle. I touch the hilt of the knife. *How dramatic.*

A black cat stirs to life in the shelf. She leaps off the shelf, startling me. I bump into the display, knocking *Damaged Hearts* from its spot.

"Whoops…"

I pick up the book. The knife is a prop, but the slice in the book is real, the pages torn through. It flutters open when I try to re-position the display, and I notice something odd.

There's a signature on the front page. I recognize it from my own signed copy. It looks like Quinn's handwriting. It just says: *I'm sorry.*

Why would she be sorry…?

Unless…?

I get a strange, creeping feeling. The black cat knocks her head against my legs. She stretches, her paws extending forward.

I scratch the top of her head. I feel like I even know this cat. *The cat's name is Behemoth*, I think to myself.

She meows at me and twitches her ears. I glance at her collar. The tag reads: *Behemoth.*

My heart is pounding. *Pounding.*

Dorian comes back. The book is tightly wrapped in nice, crisp wrapping paper. He sets it on the table in front of me.

"Merry Christmas. Don't say I never did anything for you."

But I'm staring at him. Really, genuinely looking at him. Passages from the novel come back to me, flashing through my head.

I gripped Poe's hips, feeling the bones underneath sharply against my palms.

His beard prickled my cheek as he sighed into my ear.

But it was his moan—a deep, uncontrolled sound that escaped him—that I loved the most.

I knew those hips. That beard. Those low moans.

"It's you," I say.

His eyebrows knit. "Sorry?"

"You. You're Poe. You're the guy in this book who sleeps with his brother's wife."

His eyes widen briefly. Then he turns away from me. He lets out a sound which is half a laugh, half a bitter sigh. "Two million copies sold," he says, "and you're the first one to crack the case. Well done, Nancy Drew."

I couldn't wrap my head around it.

The book boyfriend who wore out my vibrator…

The dominant of my dreams…

…Is my real life submissive.

"I'm…you…how…?"

"Take a breath, Dove," he reminds me.

I try. I breathe. In, out.

He leans against his desk. He grips the wood, muscles in his arms flexing as they tense. But his eyes remain trained on me. Observing my mini-melt down. Finally, he relents.

"Alright," he says. He pulls out his phone, pulls up his timer app, and sets it on the desk beside him. "Should we play our game? You have five minutes to ask me anything, and then we put this subject to bed for the night. How does that sound?"

It sounds like a start, I want to say. But I'll take it. For now. I nod.

He clicks the *start* button, and the timer starts ticking down.

"You're Poe," I repeat. I just need this confirmed. About twenty times.

He nods, slowly, and gives me the truth. "Poe was my scene name. Mark is my brother. Quinn is my…" He looks off, losing eye contact. "Well. My mistake. The worst mistake I ever made in my life. And now, thanks to her retelling, that mistake is memorialized forever." His gaze finds me again.

"But. You know. She sends me signed copies to sell. Quite generous."

The acid in his tone is dark, venomous, and laced with repressed rage.

I can't stop staring at him. He's a puzzle and I'm trying to put the two pieces together: could Poe and Dorian really be the same person?

More than the reveal, I'm surprised by my response. I'm shocked, but…not as shocked as I *should be*.

There's some part of it that *makes sense*. It fits. The way he knew how to negotiate our play sessions as soon as we started talking. The way he could hold my gaze unflinchingly. The way he trained me to give him what *he* wanted, how *he* wanted it. The way he coached me to be his perfect domme.

Even in his brattiest moments, or when he was at his most desperate, somehow I always knew…*this is a man in control who wants to be controlled.*

"Was it true?" I ask. "What she wrote."

Those blue eyes lift, meeting my gaze. "A lot of it," he admits. "Not all of it."

"Which parts?"

The edges of his eyes crinkle. A bitter, wry amusement. But his jaw flexes, a ripple of anger underneath. "You want Poe's version of the story?"

I shake my head. "I want Dorian's version."

The tense muscle in his jaw relaxes. He exhales a small, tight sigh, his rage dispersing with it. When he speaks again, his voice is calmer. More controlled. "I was going through my own mid-life crisis, I suppose. I had the bookstore. I was into the kink community. And I was open about it.

"Meanwhile, my brother—Mark. He had the whole package. Beautiful house, beautiful wife, beautiful life. It was hard to look at him and all his accomplishments and not feel like I was a step behind. Like life had run away without me and now I was just wasting my best years.

"And then…Quinn gave me a proposal. Things were… falling apart with her and Mark. They'd just had their first baby and they weren't connecting. She wanted to re-kindle things with him. Learn something new. And she wanted me to teach her how to do it. She knew I was part of the BDSM community. On paper, it made sense. I was safe. I was family. She was trying to reconnect with my brother. We established our hard limits: no sex. It was also supposed to be…platonic. But." He folds his arms over his chest protectively. "I lost control."

"You fell in love."

He grimaces. "Yeah. I did."

A silence. A breath for that. I feel a deep, outpouring of empathy. I know what it's like to fall in love with the wrong person. *Been there, done that.*

"What happened next?"

He inhales. There's a shake to his breath, like rusty wheels trying to get moving again. "My brother found out. The whole thing unraveled very quickly. She went back to him— as she should." His eyes met mine again. Pleading for under-standing. "I got a black eye and a threat to never come near their family again. But the books came out. She wrote about it. Everything we'd done. Every time I'd played with her and fucked her behind my brother's back. For the world to see. I lost friends. My family—my parents, my extended family— all of them cut me off. I was the villain in her story, after all." Quieter, he adds: "Rightfully so."

"Did you ever try to explain it? Tell them your side?"

"And say what? I was in charge. The entire time. It was my responsibility to stay in control and I fucked up."

"You can't…punish yourself forever."

A small, bitter smile curves his lips. "Why not, when it feels so good?"

I examine him. "So…just to be clear. You took her to the Seeker's Club…?"

He nods. "I knew Phantom. Princess. But I haven't been there in years. I've worked very, very hard to separate myself from that phase in my life. I stopped playing. I stopped dominating. It all just…reminded me too much of every terrible thing I'd done."

In my brain, I'm trying to fit the timelines together. Dorian stopped going to the club around about when I started. We must have been ships in the night.

What would've happened if we'd run into each other then…?

"When was the last time you saw her?"

He shifts from one foot to the other. His arms tighten around his chest. "A year ago. We…rebounded. For a night. I don't recommend it."

"A year ago. So right before…"

"Right before I started messaging you. Yes."

A sting of jealously, unbidden, whips up through my chest. The question—the *real* question I want to ask—comes pouring out before I can stop it: "Do you still love her?"

His phone chimes. The timer goes off. Five minutes is up.

I'm crushed.

His finger taps a button, silencing the chimer. But then he answers my question anyway. "I did once. Very much. But now I see it for what it was. Obsession. Not love. Every time I think about her now, I cringe. I hate the person I was with her. I was so desperate to be loved by her, I abandoned my own firmly held beliefs. I lost my brother. My family. Everything that was important to me. I lost myself. That…the fact that I gave up so much of myself for her…that's what makes me angry at the end of the day. I'm furious with myself."

I settle into my skin. "I get it."

The blue eyes meet mine. Something like hope in them. Shocked that someone would listen to his side of the story, maybe. "You do?"

"Yeah…when I think about who I was with Shawn, I just feel…embarrassed. I let him walk all over me. I let him take so much. I don't recognize that woman anymore. I'm just so fucking—"

"—Angry," he says, finishing our thoughts.

Our eyes connect. There's a strange energy here now.

A new understanding between us.

Damaged hearts indeed. Our hearts share the same bruises. The same ugly, shameful scars. I close the distance between us. I put my hand to his chest. I can feel that broken heart of his. It's beating so fast against my palm.

"Your heart," I tell him. "It's pounding."

His jaw locks. He's revealed too much of himself tonight, and now he's shutting away again. But I don't let him. I lean my body against his.

"Book two," I continue. "Chapter fifteen. The scene where you fuck her in your bookstore. True or false?"

He swallows, that knot in his throat bobbing. "True."

We're so close now. I touch my forehead to his. He exhales, and his breath shakes against my lips. "We're taking control of the narrative. I'm rewriting your story." I move my hands to his belt. I undo it and the metal clicks in my hands. "Now be a good boy and put your palms behind your back."

For once, Dorian obeys without question.

He plants his palms on the desk on either side of him, locking them in place. I slide my hands down his form. I push his sweater up, exposing that slim midriff. I dance my fingertips over the bare skin, the soft, dark hairs around his naval, and his muscle contract under my touch. His belt hisses as I slide it from his hips. I reach behind him, wrap the belt around his wrists, and tighten it. It's not particularly sturdy, but it will hold him back. For now.

I nestle into the crook of his neck like a cat. He has a clean smell, like aftershave and shampoo, and it mixes in nicely with the heady, earthy smell of paperbacks all around us. I kiss the space underneath his ear, and then draw his earlobe briefly through my teeth.

"Do you want me, Dorian?" I ask.

His breath is light. "More than anything, boss."

I bite my lip. "Do you want to know what I think?"

He's panting against his teeth. This isn't sub space. This is Dorian barely holding onto to his hinges. And I have him… right where I want him.

"She might've loved you. But I *see* you. I know you. I know every fucked up part of you, and I'm still here. And I think that scares the hell out of you."

I nudge my thigh against his groin. He lets out a heavy groan. He's rock hard against my leg. "Oh, yeah. You feel really…*really* scared."

I press a line of kisses down his throat and lower myself to my knees. I nestle against the happy trail above his groin and nibble him there.

"Give me a color," I tell him.

"Green," he growls. "Bright fucking green."

His zipper hisses as I pull it down. "Tell me to stop."

"Stop."

"Now like you mean it."

"Please," his voice is strained. "Please, stop."

I pull up my dress and get to my knees. I yank his pants down his thighs and I nestle against the soft cotton of his dark briefs. There's a patch of wet where he's leaking for me. I run the flat of my tongue against the cotton and he shivers.

"So you don't want me to take you in my mouth…and suck you until you explode?"

He moans. "Anything but that."

"Too bad. You're mine, and I want to worship you."

I pulls his briefs down, freeing his cock. My mouth waters. Oh, god. I want this. I *really* want this. I'm seized with a need to cherish this cock. I want to bring Dorian to his knees with more pleasure than Quinn or any woman or any toy in his chest or even his right hand has ever given him.

I want to rewrite his DNA and tangle it up in mine until we're so entwined, he can't even remember who he was before he met me.

The floor bites my knees in a wonderful way. I keep my eyes on his face, watching his reactions. I wrap my fingers around him, feeling the powerful muscle grow hot and stiff. I press my tongue against him and slowly run it all the way up to the tip, until I taste the salt of him.

Dorian's head drops back. His biceps twitch, but his hands are bound behind his back. His eyebrows pinch and he exhales under his breath a swift, reverent: "Jesus fucking Christ, boss."

A single swipe of my tongue, and I've almost undone him.

My poor, pent-up boy.

I shift on my knees. My nipples are chaffing, rock hard underneath my dress. My blood is hot, and there's a puddle in my panties, but I can't be bothered with that now. Not when I'm far too absorbed in the task at hand. I've spent the past four months getting a fucking *PhD* in Dorian's body language, so I already know each one of his pain and plea-sure points. Holding him in place, I savor the red, swollen head of his cock. I tease him against the puffy swell of my lips, and give small, worship licks to that angry vein right underneath the tip of him.

He moans again—those unrestrained, deep moans I know so well. I love how vocal he is—like he isn't afraid to want. I wrap my lips around the head of him and suck him down into my mouth. He's big, so big, and it's been—well—over a year since I've done this. So I give myself grace and go slowly, taking him in bit by bit.

It doesn't matter how slow I go, though. He's running too hot, already furiously close, I can tell by the way he throbs and pulses with each pass of my lips. I slide myself up and down, familiarizing myself with his size, and then I go for it, pushing down as far as I can take him. But there's *so much* of him, and even as I relax my throat, opening to him and exhaling through my nose, there's still enough left to wrap my hand around the base of him and grip.

I forgot how much I like this. I forgot how much I really, genuinely *like* sucking dick.

I let myself enjoy him. I slide myself up and down him, licking and sucking, teasing and stroking. He's noisy at first, moaning and swearing, words like *boss* and *Dove* pouring from his lips. But I know he's far gone when he suddenly stills. I rest my hand to his abdomen and I can feel the muscles there, hard and clenched. His jaw is tight. He's breathing through his teeth in short, controlled breaths. Trying so, so hard to be a good boy for me.

Until he breaks.

"Boss," he warns, his voice heavy and thick as velvet. "I'm close."

"Mmhm," I tell him, not letting up. "Give it to me." I bob my head faster, suck harder, giving him no choice but to unravel.

He moans and obeys, unleashing down my throat. I feel him swell, twitch, and then there's that lovely hit of salt that fills my mouth so quickly my nose and eyes burn. I swallow him down, flexing my throat around him, gulping as quickly as I can, even as I feel some spill over the edge of my lips.

I start to pull back, but—

Dorian's fingers suddenly thread through my hair and grip.

The belt hangs uselessly around one wrist. Now, he's got a fistful of my hair in his hand.

"Where do you think you're going?" he asks, and his voice is a growl. Low. Dark. Different. He cups the back of my head, shoving me back down his cock. Something turns in his expression, like twisting a key. His fingers tighten at the back of my head, locking in. He grips his cock and pushes it against my lips, back into my open, waiting mouth. "I'm not finished with you."

I choke.

Spit slides down my cheek. I inhale sharply through my nose, mouth and throat stuffed, full of *him*. He grinds his hips against my face, fucking my throat, still rock hard, and it sends a surge through me.

My brain completely shuts off. Bliss rockets through me as I let myself be used in a way I haven't in so long, and it feels *so goddamn good* that my cunt clenches, tightens, and pulses. I whimper, clutching his hips as he rides out his pleasure against my messy, dripping face and I feel my own orgasm flood my panties—this agonizing, ache that I've never felt before, coming without even being touched, without any friction, just from the fucking *joy* of this man's cock in my throat...

I don't know how he has anything left—I don't know how much a single man can give—but he gives it to me. All of it. Anything I ask for, he'll give me. I know that now. He pumps into my face—brutal, angry—my breath coming in clipped, short inhales through my nose, my chest tight from the lack of oxygen, my head spinning. I cry out, my scream muffled, my face trapped against his pelvis, as I throb. It's so good, I'm crying. He lets me fall apart, his grip in my hair keeping my body upright, as he moans—almost a pained sound—and pours another mouthful of salt into me.

I don't know how long I'm there, sucking like my life depends on it. But gently, he uses his thumb to unhook my jaw and pulls himself from me, leaving me with an empty pop. My face feels wet and sticky. I gulp in a breath. It's the cleanest air I've ever tasted.

He tucks away then kneels down in front of me.

We're on the same level now. His eyes are so blue. Electric. Humming. "Did you swallow?"

I shake my head. My mouth is full, otherwise I'd tell him: *you didn't give me permission, and I'm a good girl.*

He presses his thumb to my bottom lip. "Give it to me."

We kiss. My tongue tangles with his, and I swap his pleasure into his mouth. He drinks from me, taking it, and when his tongue returns to my mouth, we taste the same. I can't tell where I end and he begins.

Our kiss breaks. Both of us are panting for air. He strikes his thumb over the edge of his mouth, cleaning himself up. "Good girl," he says.

Wait…shouldn't I be saying that? To him?

Instead, my insides melt. Everything in me melts. A year's worth of self-protective, brick walls come crumbling down into so much dust around me.

"Oh," I whisper. "Oh, no." My voices is shaky. All of me is shaky.

"I know," he says. His voice is calm, and he's so big, so strong, and I need that right now because I'm small, so small. "Come here."

I want to.

I need to.

But I look up at him and suddenly, I see Shawn. The dark eyes. The charming grin. Those strong hands that reach out and say *you can trust me*, but hurt instead. The devil in sheep's clothing.

Suddenly, I can't move, think, or speak.

Shawn's eyebrows knit. "You okay?"

"I'm…" Throat tight. Words struggling to escape. "I'm… um…sorry…I have to…where's your bathroom?"

He points to the back of the bookstore. "Next to the owl."

"Thanks." I scramble to my feet and rush away for him before he can try to pull me back again. I find the bathroom cornered off next to the children's section. The children's section has a large mural on the wall of an owl in a tree with a lopsided rainbow sprouting from the owl's wing. I zip into the bathroom, close the door, and brace myself on the sink. The porcelain feels cold under my fingers. I grip it tight, close my eyes, and just focus on my breaths.

In, out. In, out.

Panic runs through my like wildfire, skipping impishly through my veins.

You're safe, I tell myself. *You're safe. Shawn's not here.*

The roaring, pounding of my heart gently starts to come down. I open my eyes. The woman in the mirror looks insane. Those softened green eyes, drunk on pleasure. Lips extra puffy, like I just used an entire bottle of hot sauce as lipstick. Hair twisted up like a sex-tornado.

My heart kicks in my chest. It's like seeing a long-lost lover for the first time and having all those feelings come flooding back, but it's *me*.

I can't help but think: *oh, there she is.*

The truth is—I loved it. Every second of it. I loved being on my knees for Dorian. I loved his fingers twisted in my hair. I loved the dark, demanding growl in his voice when he sank deeper into my mouth.

So why this, now? Why the trembling panic after?

I pull myself together. I rinse my face, cleaning the sweet, stickiness that dribbled down my chin and throat. I gargle and spit. Then I drop my pants, and sit on the toilet. Gingerly, I touch myself. I'm all slippery down there, swollen. Even the lightest touch takes the breath from my lungs.

My panties are ruined. I mop them up the best I can.

I do the best I can to touch up my makeup and comb my fingers through my hair. When I exit the bathroom, I find Dorian in a similar state—in disarray, desperately trying to look normal.

Our eyes meet. He gives me a small smile.

Immediately, relief floods my chest.

It's Dorian again. Not Shawn. Just Dorian.

"All good, boss?" he asks.

Those blue eyes. The gentle concern in his voice.

My sweet, submissive Dorian.

I'm safe again.

I exhale a deep breath, coming back into my body.

"All good," I confirm with a thumbs up. "But we should catch up with the crew. They're probably wondering where we are."

"Right."

We're both quiet for a minute after that, sinking into the weight of our silence. I'm so aware of everything around me suddenly. The bookstore. The dents in my knees. The tangles in my hair.

Maybe neither of us are completely done with the people we once were.

"I see a taxi," Dorian says suddenly. He runs out the door, hand lifted. Dorian gives a sharp whistle—that charming, weird little quirk of his—and the cabbie pulls to a stop.

I exhale a small breath. Whatever *this* was…it's time to rejoin the world.

I exit the bookstore and the cold blast of air wakes me the fuck up.

11

FUCK

Dorian. **Now.**

Fuck.

Fuck. Shitty—fuck, fuck, *FUCK*.

Outside, I am smooth as glass, composed in the backseat of the taxi cab, watching the red and green and gold lights of New York City slide across the window pane.

Inside, a brass band of self-hatred is dancing on top of my fucking gravestone.

Here Lies Dorian Lennon. That Fucking Idiot Who Did The Thing He Swore He'd Never Do Again. Rest in Pieces, You Piece of—

"That's the ugliest owl I've ever seen in my life," Dove says.

I blink out of my spiral. "What is?"

"In your bookstore. The owl on the wall."

"Ah. That. I got drunk one night and thought I was Picasso. It turns out I'm just..."

"Pi-can't-o?"

A light chuckle leaves me. "Yes. Exactly."

She's trying to fill in the quiet that's settled in between us. We're both trying to shake off the fact that something has *changed* between us. The silence is punctuated only by the irritating video screen that informs us of the weather, today's lottery numbers, and invites us to play Tic-Tac-Toe while we ride.

I hate these pre-programmed videos, but I find myself watching it anyway because I can't look at her. I can barely stand the glimpse of her out of the corner of my vision. Because now, when I look at her, I can only see those swollen lips wrapped around my cock.

What non-kink people don't understand is that *Dominance* and submission and these power games we play is more than arousal.

When I saw Dove on her knees, with that sub-space, dreamy look in her eyes, it unlocked something in me.

Yes, my dick got harder.

Yes, my heart swelled in my chest.

But it's more. *More* than that. Because the Dominant side of me—that part I've kept flattened down at the bottom of my soul like a very, very neatly organized travel bag—suddenly sprang back to life, Jack-in-the-box style.

And now, *I can't stop thinking about her on her knees.*

I can't stop thinking about her soft, sweet moans. I can't stop thinking about the way she didn't even hesitate—she just took me in deeper, like her mouth was made to accept my cock. Most of all, I can't stop thinking about those eyes.

Those *fuck me up, sir* eyes.

I can't stop thinking about how perfect it would be to make her mine.

I curl my fingers, nails digging into the pliable rubbery fabric coating the door handle. I want to rip it apart. I want to hear the fabric whine. I want to yank it from its home.

I haven't let my Dominant side out to play in years. *Years.* Except for that one night, that one fucked up night I swore I wouldn't repeat again. And now it's chasing me like an animal. This feeling is like snorting cocaine, following it with an energy drink, and then biting down on a live grenade and pulling the pin.

Fuck.

Goddammit.

Shit.

I want Dove to slap me. I want her to get me on my knees. I want her to tell me *I'm* her good boy. I want her to control me, because right now, if I've proven anything tonight, it's this:

I can't control myself.

Not around Dove, anyway.

I made that clear the second I flooded her mouth with pleasure and grabbed her by the back of her head to finish it *my way.*

I could leave. Politely bow out. Tell her I've had a great evening, go home, masturbate as many times as my dick can handle until I pass out—

"You know I was an art student in previous life," Dove continues. "I could touch up your ugly owl for you."

A wry grin slips over my mouth. I push my hand down my thigh, ironing out a wrinkle in the pants. "Look at you, touching up all my terrible mistakes."

Dove turns her head towards the window. The city lights flash across her face, tones of yellow and blue.

"I think that's part of getting older," she says.

"What? Watching yourself make the same mistakes over and over again?"

"No...learning to forgive yourself. Even when it's hard. Especially when it's hard."

I have nothing to say to that.

Forgiveness instead of punishment. What a novel idea.

I watch the numbers tick upward on the cabbie's meter. The cabbie keeps his eyes on the road. Cabbies are a bit like priests—they've heard everything, and they repeat nothing. Code of silence, I guess.

"It's kind of funny," Dove says.

"What is?"

"Well...I used to be a submissive. And you used to be a dominant. Look at us now."

"Would you like to know a secret?" I ask her.

Dove nods.

I tell her, "You were my first domme."

Dove's eyes meet mine. They go a little wide, and there's something like pride in her expression. I can tell I've pleased her. That feels good, at least. A sliver of serotonin in Dove's smile. Then she cocks her head and says, "Well, that's not much of a secret. You're a terrible submissive."

I can't help it. I laugh.

Dove has that effect on me.

She makes me happy even when I'd rather stew in my own self-loathing.

We've rolled into Brooklyn. The cab slows, trying to find the venue.

When we get out of this taxi, we'll be back with her friends, and back in the chaos. If I want to say something, I'd better say it now.

I find my lips moving without consent from my brain.

"At the bookstore," I say, "I took it too far. I'm sorry. I lost control and—"

"Red," she says suddenly.

I blink. Did she just...*safe word*? In the middle of a conversation?

"Ah...what?"

"*Red,*" she repeats. "Don't you dare ever apologize for

what just happened. I won't be another reason you hate yourself. *That* is my hard limit."

My mouth goes completely dry. I'm stunned into silence.

She sees you. Even when you don't want to be seen.

She knows you. Better than you know yourself.

I've never, ever been seen like this. I want to resist it. I want to pull away. I want to hole up inside my—what does my sister call it?—my *Dorian-shell,* and yet—

And. Yet.

There's also a part of me that wants to follow the light at the end of the tunnel. That wants to hope. That wants to see this bizarre night through.

The cab stops. Dove gets out. "Are you coming?"

"Yes, boss."

I take a breath, steel myself, and pay the cab driver.

Once I've exited the cab, however, I wonder if we've made a mistake with the address. We're in Red Hook, right by the waterfront, and the river looks black from here, the skyline across the way glittering. A redbrick warehouse looms in front of us, looking very much abandoned, with tufts of weeds and rock and trash sprouting out from the sidewalk around it.

"Are you sure this is the right place?" I ask Dove.

The taxi hasn't left yet. I could still grab it.

She points ahead. "There's Phantom!"

Sure enough, like a mirage in the desert—a blue light illuminates from a steel door down the street. A broad-shouldered bouncer balances on a stool and, beside him, there's Phantom, bundled up in his thick sweater and knitted hat.

When he approach, he gives us the standard, New Yorker greeting—a curt nod. "You found us," he says.

"They kick you out already?" Dove teases.

Phantom's smile is pinched. "It's a little much for me in there. I'm taking a breather."

The bouncer has tattoos dotted all over his face and a thick beard to keep him warm. It's a twenty-dollar fee to enter, but Phantom has apparently charmed the icicles off his heart and he waves us in for free for being "friends of a friend."

Phantom was right: it's *a lot*. The second we enter, we're met with a blast of hot air that makes my layers of thick clothes immediately unbearable. The whole place smells like sweaty bodies and that tangy scent of bubble-mixture. It's a party in here, an explosion of neon graffiti on the walls, flashing lights, glitter bombs, and half-naked bodies jumping to pounding pop music on the dance floor.

A woman shouts something at me through the open window in the box office beside me. "What?" I ask.

"Your coat!" she points to us. "You gotta check it!"

Ironically, the woman working at coat check isn't wearing a coat—she's barely wearing anything at all, with a strappy corset covering the bare minimum and a face full of sparkly makeup. Dove shoves her beanie in the arm of her coat and I pull my coat off as I hand both over to the woman, exchanging our items for a paper ticket.

Then she hands over two soft pillows. One has rubber ducks sewn on it. The other is pink with stars. "Have fun!" she says.

I hold a pillow out to Dove. She looks at me curiously. "What's this for?"

"Absolutely no idea. In case we need to nap?"

She snorts a laugh, takes the pink pillow, and tucks it under her arm.

What are we getting ourselves into?

We move through pillars plastered with old, ripped band posters to make our way to the bar. I notice everyone is in a state of undress, and they all have pillows of their own, some more ornately decorated than others.

I get us drinks—two Jack and Cokes, I don't trust their wine selection—and can barely shout the drink order to the bartender over the din of the noise. Somehow, though, Ophelia's shriek carries when she sees us.

"Where the fuck've you been!" Ophelia bounces over. She's stripped out of her clothes like many of the other degenerates here, her shirt gone with the wind, with only a strappy black bra covering her chest. Princess is with her, and both women are grinning ear to ear and covered in sparkly glitter. Ophelia puts her hands on Dove's shoulders. "I thought you got eaten alive by subway rats."

"Not yet, but good guess," Dove says.

Ophelia squints at her friend. Her eyes flicker over Dove. "Eaten by some other rat, maybe," she says, lifting her eyebrows at me.

The two women clearly know each other too well. It's clear she's read our sins all over Dove, even after we pulled ourselves together. *I guess I'll just squeak myself out...*

"Did you find the ornament?" Dove asks, changing the topic.

Ophelia rolls her eyes dramatically. "*Fuck* the ornament! Check out the battleground!"

The...*what*?

The points to a busy space beyond the dancefloor and my eyes try to make sense of what I'm seeing.

It is, in a way, the equivalent of a giant bouncy castle...for adults. The floor is covered with an inflated material, the matching walls bouncing with movement. The people in the large enclosure are a flurry of skin, glitter, and activity. And they're all smacking each other with pillows, screaming and laughing.

"Is that...a giant pillow fight?" Dove asks.

"Yes!" Ophelia shouts. "You have to get in! It's so much fun!"

Dove grins. I see the temptation in her eyes, the hungry way she watches the chaos, but she shakes her head and calls back over the din: "Maybe in a minute. We just got drinks!"

"Chug them while we put on your war paint."

Ophelia removes a small tube of makeup from her bra—how do women keep so many items stuffed in their bra? It's a true magic trick. She hands it over to Princess. "You take Dove," Ophelia says. "I've got this one." She's looking at me when she says it. This must be what a prey animal feels like in an open field. Ophelia corners me, tugs a chair from the bar, and points to it. "Sit."

I don't argue. My eyes flit to Dove (*help!*) but she only looks amused, shrugs, and lets Princess paint her face in gold glitter.

Ophelia crouches down in front of me. She puts her knee on my thigh, half in my lap, and squeezes a dollop of glitter-paint onto her finger.

"Consent?" she asks.

"Granted." Anything for Dove.

The face paint is cold as she smears it on my cheeks. She drops her voice to something covert and serious. "You and me need to have a conversation."

"About…?"

"About how I'm going to kick your ass."

Seems fair, but—"Why, exactly?"

"Dove is a badass. Got that? But she's also a sweetheart. She falls in love easily and she gets fucked over easily. Are you following me?"

"Yes, but—"

"She doesn't need a boyfriend right now. Or a significant other. What she needs now is an unattached, emotionally distant dildo. Which I thought you were."

"Put that on my gravestone."

"Except I've been watching you. The way you look at her

with those big, eager puppy eyes. I need to you turn off the puppy eyes."

I nod slowly. She clearly sees me as a threat right now, and she's not going to hear me if I tell her that hurting Dove is the *last* thing on my mind. "I'll do my best."

She narrows her eyes at me. "I've got my eyes on you, dildo."

"I can see that."

"Dildo-Baggins."

"Can I get you some water?"

She snaps the cap back on her tube. She climbs off me and spins around to Dove. My face feels wet and messy with whatever Ophelia put on it. Princess is much more exacting about her lines, and Dove has a few nice, precise glitter-swirls on her face.

"Break!" Ophelia punches her fist in the air. "Let's fucking go!" She grabs her pillow and lets out a roar loud enough to wake the Valkyries. Princess follows her and the two dive back into the fray, smacking each other with pillows as they go.

Dove comes over to me. Her fingers slide into my hair. It grounds me. "That's a good look on you," she tells me.

I tilt my head up to look at her. "She's going to be fun to pick up off the floor later."

"It's her birthday," Dove says. "She can get as sloppy as she wants. Those are the rules."

Her hand comes up, cupping the side of my neck. Her thumb very gently puts pressure in that hollow space between my throat and my jaw, reminding me who is in charge, and my brain activity immediately kicks down a couple notches.

"Be nice," she tells me.

I am not *nice*, I am the furthest thing from nice, but I can be obedient, and the inner-brat in me shuts the fuck up with Dove's hand on my throat.

"Dove?" A man's voice. From the Mad Max fever dream of the chaotic bar, a couple emerges and approaches us. He's a burly redhead with his arm around a petite blonde, her hair pulled back into a too-tight ponytail. He has this wide, wolfish grin when his eyes scan over Dove.

I stand, immediately putting myself between him and Dove.

I don't like the way he's looking at her. It sends my nerves on end.

"Holy shit," he says. "It is you."

Dove's hand moves to her mouth. Her voice comes out like a bird chirp. "Hey…uh. Holy shit! Shawn. What are you doing here?"

Shawn. The name is like an injection of ice water in my veins.

I know all about Shawn. The so-called dominant who claimed Dove, played with Dove, and broke Dove's heart.

Fucking. Shawn.

He seems to think it's okay to pull Dove into a hug, and she lets him, stiffly resting her body briefly against his like one of those plastic dolls that won't bend.

I am already in a half-primal state and my mind swims with vivid images of grabbing him by his curly hair and ripping his throat to sinewy threads between my teeth just for the crime of touching her.

Luckily for him, he pulls away, takes a step back, and stares at her. That shit-eating grin still stamped across his face.

"You look…different," he says.

"Yeah." She nods. "You too."

"Good for you."

Her eye twitches, like that phrase triggers a deep, unsettled madness.

I slip my arm around Dove, resting my hand on the small of her back. *This is mine.*

Dove reaches back and puts her hand on my chest, as though she's just remembering I exist. "This is Dorian."

Shawn's eyes flicker over me, sizing me up. "Cool. Hey, dude." He extends his hand. I take it.

Fuck you, you don't deserve to breathe the same air as Dove. Touch her again and I'll rip your hands off and shove them down your throat. I attempt to convey all of this through the grip of my hand while I smile through gritted teeth.

When I release him from my fuck-you hand shake, he puts his hand on the woman's shoulder. "This is my girlfriend, Ginger."

"Nice to meet you!" she says. I was too angry to see her before. I take stock of her now. She's all smiles, with this little black band around her throat, a pink heart at the middle. She has this clueless look in her eyes that's, honestly, almost heartbreaking as she glances between the two of them. "How do you know each other?"

"We used to date." Shawn shrugs, like it's nothing.

My anger tastes like battery acid on my tongue.

Dove nods to the bouncy castle. "Are you guys going in?"

"It looks fun!" Ginger says, glancing back at the pile of humans bouncing around.

"Yeah," Shawn snorts, "if you're twelve."

He doesn't even notice how the light goes out at Ginger's eyes. My heart really does go out to the poor thing. It's like watching a baby seal twist around in a bear trap. *Fuck you, you fucking monster.*

"Well, spank my ass and take me to Claire's, because I'm definitely going in," Dove says.

I slip my hand to the back of Dove's neck. "Absolutely. I'll try anything once."

Dove leans into me. We're being extra touchy-feely in front of them. "He's a saint."

"She's a killer."

I kiss the side of her head, and under the pounding music, I whisper in Dove's ear, "Want to make him regret his life?"

She doesn't speak, but she responds affirmatively with a, "Mmhm."

"Unhinge your jaw when I kiss you."

I clutch Dove's chin, tilt her upwards, and claim her in a deep, possessive kiss.

She initially goes stiff with surprise, but then she melts into me. Obediently, she unlocks her jaw, letting my tongue invade her. I taste her, swiping my tongue against hers. My blood's too hot, my grip too tight, my kiss too rough. But Dove loves it and she lets out a soft, quiet moan that's for me, and only me.

Mine, I want to say. *Mine, and look what you gave up, you fucking idiot.*

When we break, we're both short of breath.

Ginger clears her throat. "Well! Nice to meet you two!"

Arm still wrapped around Dove, I say, "Merry Christmas, Ginger." *Not Shawn. Just Ginger.*

"Merry Christmas!" Ginger says jovially.

Shawn looks sour. I've won.

"See you around," Shawn says. He's looking directly at Dove when he says it. It feels like a command, not a request.

No. No, he won't.

They break away from us and I try to guess at Dove's mood. Her expression is flat, but her breath is hitched, and I can't tell if she's about to have a panic attack or scream.

I drop my voice so only she can hear. "Are you okay?"

"No. Not even slightly." She wraps her lips around her

straw and sucks her drink. Hard. She sucks up half the drink before she says: "She's wearing my collar. That bitch was wearing my collar."

Ah.

The collar. The sign of ownership in the kink community.

I can't imagine the chaos that's rattling around inside of Dove at this moment.

I can't make this better, so I ask, "What do you need?"

She's not looking at me. Her eyes lock on the pillow fight arena. She lifts a finger from her glass, pointing. "Dorian, do you know what this is?"

"A pillow fight?"

"No. It's permission to *rage*. You have rage. I have rage. We need this—no. We deserve this. Come rage with me."

I haven't engaged in a pillow fight in—well. Maybe ever.

But there's a frantic look in Dove's eyes, and I know she needs this.

"Come on," she says. "Growl. Like this." She bares her teeth and lets out an animal sound from deep in her throat.

I match her energy. I snarl back.

She looks pleased. "Good boy." She snaps her fingers. "Now grab your ducks and let's fuck this place up."

1 2

———————

THE FEATHER IS MIGHTIER

Dove. **Now.**

I kill my drink, grip my pink pillow, and get ready to rumble.

I saw Shawn twice tonight.

Once, in a hallucinatory nightmare after giving the best blowjob of my life.

And now, *here*, in the flesh.

He's haunting me, and his presence has me physically shaking with anger. With hurt. With emotions I can't even begin to digest.

I need to bleed these demons, or I'm going to scream.

We leave our shoes on the floor and Dorian takes my hand to help me up onto into the "ring." The mattress below is an inflatable thing and it bounces when I step up onto it. There are so many people on it already, sweaty, half-naked bodies whacking each other with pillows, laughing, giddy with the *play* of it all.

It's what I used to love about going to the club: it was a place that gave you permission to be as freaky as you wanted.

It was a release. A release I badly need right now.

I spot familiar faces in the crowd. Ophelia and Princess are smacking each other with pillows, laughing too hard to stand up. Carver is taking it very seriously and smacks someone so thoroughly with the pillow, the other guy tumbles off the mattress.

The second I'm in, I get whacked from behind. I yelp and turn around.

There's Dorian, holding his duck-covered pillow and wearing a smirk.

Oh, it's on.

We pillow-fight, the soft material smacking me in the face, on my body. I bounce around on the platform, trying to stay upright. When I tumble, Dorian tumbles with me. I rain unholy pillow-hell on him until he's forced to scramble away. A dinosaur-pillow comes at me, and a stranger takes Dorian's place.

I become a pillow-warrior. I'm jumping from place to place, wielding my pillow indiscriminately. It feels *so good* to let this energy out and I find myself getting too into it. I roar like a warrior on a battle field as I spin and take out my latest victim.

She squeaks. "Mercy!" she calls out, but she's laughing.

I come to a dead stop.

It's Ginger. She's entered the fray, and now she's at my mercy.

The anger rises up again, hot and intense.

She looks so much *like me*. Well. *Old me.*

That bleached blonde hair.

My black collar with the pink heart in the center.

Those submissive, I'll-do-whatever-you-want eyes.

I could end her. Take her out. Right now. Show her the full force of my rage. I lift my pillow to take her down. I get ready to whack her, but...

I can't.

Ginger doesn't fight back. Instead, she lifts her arms to protect herself and squeals with laughter, bracing for an impact that never comes. When I don't hit her, she looks up at me and blinks curiously.

Something in me switches. The rage is gone, swept right out of my body, and all I can feel now is this intense, aching heartbreak.

Heartbreak for Ginger. Heartbreak for *me*. For that innocent, love-struck woman who wanted to believe in good people. Who dared to *trust*.

Is that such a crime?

I drop my pillow. Instead, I find myself wrapping my arms around Ginger, yanking her into a tight hug.

She gives a little squeak but then wraps her arms back around me, accepting my strange affection.

"It's not your fault," I tell her.

"What?" We can barely hear each other over the chaos around us.

"*Run,*" I say into her ear. "You're perfect. You deserve so, so much better than that asshole."

Her eyebrows knit, that pretty smile falling from her face. She looks rattled.

"Sorry," she says, "I have to…I should…"

She stumbles backwards. I catch her to keep her from falling, but she pulls away from me. I watch as she climbs out of the arena and rushes back to the bar. Back to Shawn.

His gaze connects with mine. My jaw goes so tight, I'm afraid I might break a tooth.

"Dove." Dorian's voice behind me. Calling me back to reality. I turn and I see concern etched into his expression. He shouts over the ruckus: "Are you okay?"

I shake my head. I'm shaking. "No."

Then he does something crazy. He gets to his knees—

which can't be easy on this bouncy inflatable. Still he kneels in front of me, and says, simply: "Show me."

It's all the permission I need.

I take everything inside me—all that rage, anger, and hurt—and I grab the edges of my pillow and hit it across his face as hard as I can.

The pillow explodes.

For a dream-like, surreal moment, everything crystalizes. Colored lights flash around me, blasting through the dark. Everyone turns my way to admire the storm cloud of chaos I've created. It's as though all this heaviness I've been carrying around inside of me for the past year is finally out, open and raw for the world to see.

And, right now, my pain is beautiful.

The feathers dance around us like snowflakes. They catch on the light, shimmering and flickering in this heady mixture of glitter and color.

For a second, everyone stops fighting. The entire crowd suddenly bursts into a round of whoops and cheers, like this is a great event. Like they're cheering for me.

Laughter breaks out of my chest. I feel lighter than I have in years.

For the first time, I'm not riddled with rage and hurt. I'm *happy*.

It's liberating.

Through the constellation of feathers, my eyes connect with Dorian's.

He stands there, just very...*Dorian*. To anyone else, he might be another face in the crowd. To me, suddenly, I see him. Every detail. The light sweat dampening those fine curls. The way his face is drawn with a bold hand—strong eyebrows and a tight beard across his jaw. Those curious blue eyes that don't leave me for a second.

He's smiling, like *he knows*. Like he's proud of me.

My heart skips, trips over itself, and falls flat on its face in my chest.

I have never fallen in love gracefully.

My love is a messy thing. Bumbling. Full of bruises, missteps, awkward moments, sticky feathers, but...*it's mine.* It's me.

And I'm ready to be completely, unapologetically me.

He looks like he's about to say something—maybe ask me if I'm okay, or congratulate me on my powerful swing—but before he can make a sound, I grab his face, pull him down, and meet his lips with mine.

We're experts at pain. Pleasure. And the aching, sexual torment that lies somewhere in between.

But this sweet, sincere intimacy between us is new.

Affection breaks over me like a fever, bursting from my chest. His skin is hot in my hands, his beard pleasantly rough against my palm. But his mouth is a soft, gentle hunger, and he meets me, kissing me back. I open, inviting him in, and I taste his tongue in my mouth, caressing mine in a way that sends a rush of heat tingling through my body, all the way down to my bare toes that curl on the inflatable floor.

We break for a breath, but we don't part. He pants lightly against my lips, and I hold him here. I don't want to be apart from him, not even an inch.

"Was that okay?" I ask.

"Yes," he says.

I nestle my nose to his. I kiss the edge of his mouth. "Do you want to take me home tonight?"

He moans quietly, as though the promise of taking me home is *enough.* "Yes," he says again.

I press one more kiss to his mouth. Then I almost say it. It almost comes out. "Dorian, I..."

...*love you.*

But before I can get the words out, a pillow smacks me in the head, so hard I nearly see stars.

"Whew!" Ophelia shouts victoriously, the offending pillow in her hand. "Gotcha!"

"Ow!" I rub what is certainly going to be a goose egg on my skull. "Bitch. There's something seriously wrong with your pillow."

"There is *not*, ya baby."

"Actually," Dorian points to her pillow, "I think there's something in there."

No, I want to plead. *Let's get back to me!* Because I had something to say, something really important, but now the moment is melting away from me like snow on my tongue, and there's nothing I can do but let the cold ice of words unsaid slide back down my throat.

Ophelia reaches into her pillow case. Sure enough, there's a round lump in the case. She shoves her hand in, hunting around, and pulls out a purple ornament.

"Ah!" she shrieks. "Found it!"

Dorian gives me a mildly exasperated, but amused look. I can only return it.

I can't speak. My heart is pounding too hard in my chest.

Ophelia pops open the ornament. She unravels the slip of paper inside and reads it out loud. *"Around and 'round we go... we spin so fast, but I won't let you go..."*

She stares off into the distance, mouthing the words a couple times, and I can practically see the gears in her hear turning. Then she shouts: "I've got it! Next stop: the Carousel Bar!"

She scampers off, nearly slipping on the inflatable in her haste. Dorian catches her elbow to help her right herself before she rushes to collect the rest of our friends.

He glances back at me. We're alone again. I could tell him now.

"The Carousel?" Dorian asks.

"Yeah, it's…a bar. In Dumbo."

"Well?" he asks. "Where to?"

Home? Or the Carousel?

I bite my lip. "We've come too far. We have to see it through now."

He nods. I expect disappointment from him, maybe, but instead, he takes my hand in his. The small intimacy makes my heart jump.

"Come on," he says. "Let's round up the rest of your friends."

* * *

It's well past midnight when we leave. We exit into the crisp, cool night and it feels like I've left a dream-world.

Dorian hands me my jacket, but I need to cool off. I hang it over my arm.

All of us are sticky, sweaty, and covered in sparkles. Everyone except for Phantom, who meets us outside. His nose slightly red from the cold; he lifts two fingers in a wave when he sees us.

"Find what you were looking for?" he asks.

Ophelia twists the riddle triumphantly between her fingers. "Carousel Bar, here we come."

"I'll get a cab."

"Wait…" Ophelia trails away from us. She skips down the sidewalk and motions for us to follow. "Come here!"

Dorian gives me a questioning look, I shrug. We follow Ophelia like rats behind the Pied Piper.

She takes us to the end of the road. It stops at the river. She leans again the metal railing and I move up beside her.

"God," she says, "it's beautiful, isn't it?"

The Manhattan skyline stretches out ahead of us. It's a

clear night, and the city sparkles. It looks like a twinkling, upside-down chandelier. The light spills across the water, which laps softly below us.

Dorian comes beside me. I lean against his body and he opens his coat to tuck me inside of it.

Carver leans over the railing. He spits into the river.

Princess wrinkles her nose. "Classy."

Carver hocks. Spits again. Laughs.

Princess rolls her eyes and pulls out her vape. As she takes a drag, she makes eye contact with Phantom, who is staring at the vape in her hand. She seems to remember herself and hides the vape back into her pocket.

I watch it all—the little movements between each of them —and my heart swells.

Family. This is what family feels like. I'd almost forgotten the feeling.

"Those city lights," Carver says, "don't fall for them. It's a trap."

Dorian, curious, bites. "What do you mean?"

Carver motions to the skyline. "I mean…you look at that and you forget the subway rats. The overpriced rent. The black mold in your bathroom. The dog shit on the sidewalks. You forget all the dirt and grime and like an idiot you just… fall in love with the city all over again."

Ophelia hums. "That's city magic, baby."

She hooks her arm in mine. I lean my head on her shoulder.

For a moment, all six of us just…go quiet and live in the silence.

The magic of it all, I guess.

The thought comes to me: *this has been a perfect night.*

Even if tomorrow is terrible. Even if Dorian and I never talk again after tonight. Even if I wake up with a hangover the size of Texas and regret every one of my decisions…*this moment is perfect.*

I must not be the only one who thinks that way, because Ophelia suddenly straightens up. "Holy shit," she says, "I almost forgot. C'mon, nerds. Picture time. Hey!" She starts back down the sidewalk and waves the bouncer over. "My dude! You seem cool. How're your photo skills?"

Ophelia manages to talk the bouncer into taking our photo. As he positions his phone to take the shot, we all move into place. Phantom gives the bouncer his phone and Ophelia bounds over to us.

"Alright, everyone! Places. Here. For reference."

She holds up her phone, displaying the picture from last year. Everyone else falls into their places: Ophelia in Phantom's arms, Princess climbing Carver's back.

In last year's picture, I'm crouched in front of Shawn, with his hand around my throat. But before I can move into place, Dorian kneels down in front of me. Which is when I realize: he's taken *my* place from last year's photo. He's letting *me* be the one in charge this time around.

He tilts his head, glancing up at me. His eyes asking, *is this okay?* "Rewriting our narratives," he explains. "Yes?"

I feel my grin slide across my lips. "Yes."

I settle in behind Dorian, the hard warmth of his body against mine. I wrap my hand snugly around his throat. I feel the muscle working as he swallows in my grip. I smile and before the flash goes off, I give him a gentle squeeze and say:

"*Good boy.*"

13

———

THE LAST STOP

Dorian. **Now.**

This is it. We've come to the last stop of the night.

This very strange, very long, very *perfect* night.

The six of us manage to squeeze into a single cab. It's a tight fit, and Princess sits on Ophelia's lap, the two of them cackling, while Dove takes mine. Carver squeezes in between them and Phantom takes shotgun. Phantom has gone quiet, his gaze trained out the window.

Dove wants me to come home with her. It's hard not to think about that with her body slotted perfectly against mine. She smells like sweat and shampoo and I wind my arm around her middle and breathe her in greedily.

My lips tingle where she kissed them, and I imagine I won't be able to shake the ghost sensation until I have her mouth back on mine where it belongs.

The Carousel Bar takes us back towards Dumbo. The ride isn't long, and the girls pile out while Phantom beats me to paying the fare. When I get out, everyone is crowded together outside a bar. The window is stripped with yellow, red and orange so you can't see inside and there's a similar circus color scheme on the lights that make up a sign hanging above that read: THE CAROUSEL BAR.

But they've stalled, and I stand beside Dove, waiting.

"Okay," Ophelia says to her friends, "before we go in…I just want to say…thank you. Seriously. For coming out. All of you. I know it's a pain in the ass because it's so close to Christmas, and we've been bouncing around all night, and you're all sweaty and tired and ready to go to bed—"

Princess yawns loudly. "Don't remind me! I should've kept my pillow!"

There's a round of chuckles before Ophelia starts up again: "It just…it's been a rough year. Rougher for some of us than others." Her eyes connect with Dove's, and I feel the connection the two women have. Dove's eyes get wet, and the two women share a small, touching smile. "But you all have always been there for me," Ophelia continues. "No matter what. I guess what I'm saying is…" she sniffs, wipes her hand under her eyes. She's drunk, that's clear. But she also means every word she's saying, and that's equally clear. "I love you bitches. Even you, Dorian."

"Love you too, Ophelia," I reply.

"Happy fucking birthday, bitch!" Dove shouts, her words echoing down the street. We all whoop, shout a round of "happy birthday," and Ophelia lights up. She laughs—this wonderful, deep-throated sound—and I can see why she and Dove have such a deep bond.

They feel everything. Deeply. It's beautiful.

Dove scoops her friend in a hug and they give each other a long, tight squeeze. Then they break and Ophelia leaves her arm around Dove.

"Alright," Ophelia says, "Let's make thirty-five the best year yet!"

She gets another round of cheers, and all of us are in a good mood, everyone feeling as if it were *their* own birthdays, too. We enter the bar on a high, and I've seen so much strangeness tonight, that the strangeness in here doesn't even phase me.

It's another toasty bar, but for good reason. The whole bar is done up to look like the inside of a circus tent, complete with yellow and red fabric streaming at a point from the ceiling. The bartenders are dressed like circus clowns and there are dancers on poles on small stages around the bar. Men and women alike, all in various circus outfits—leotards, burlesque dresses.

We attract some attention ourselves—not because we look anything like the circus crowd, but because we come in shouting and cheering, a chorus of laughter.

But then I nearly collide with Ophelia. I stop short, resting my hand on her shoulder to keep myself from smacking into her.

She's come to a sudden stop. The smile has dropped completely from her face, and she's gone as still as a rabbit staring down the jaws of a wolf.

I follow the line of her gaze to a pair at the bar.

A bald, tan man with a sleeve of tattoos is kissing a tiger woman. I say *tiger woman* because she's dressed in a stripped one-piece with long, black "claws." Her painted-on tiger nose has left a charcoal-smear across his cheek as they tangle tongues.

"What," Ophelia says, "the *fuck*."

The man's eyes fly open. He extracts his tongue from the tiger woman and leaps up so quickly, she falls from his lap with a yowl that sounds not unlike a cat with its tail caught underfoot.

"Ophelia," he says.

"Brody," she replies.

"Brody?" I clarify.

"Brody," Dove growls, and rolls up her sleeves.

I put my hand on her shoulder, halting her from ripping the offending man to pieces with her bare hands.

"Oh, *shit,*" Princess says under her breath. There are mini bags of popcorn at the bar and she hastily grabs one, stress eating as she watches the drama unfold.

The tiger woman gets up, brushes herself off, and starts backing away, sensing she's been outnumbered. Brody, meanwhile, pulls a half-grin and lifts his arms.

"Babe! What're you doing here?"

"Following your stupid clues around all night. Or did you forget that it's my fuckin birthday?"

He blinks. "Oh. Yeah. Happy birthday."

"Happy birthday? Happy *birthday!* Making out with another woman on my goddamn fucking birthday—that kind of happy birthday?"

"We were just…hanging out…"

"Hanging out? Hanging *out!*"

What follows is painful to witness. Ophelia has had this whole, entire night built up to this moment. Now, it's hard to watch it crash down around her as her birthday night dissolves into a screaming match between her and her boyfriend.

Fed up, Ophelia swivels around and leaves the bar. Dove follows quick at her heels with the rest of their friends. Brody starts after her, but I quickly grab his arm.

"I wouldn't," I tell him.

He yanks away from me and sneers. "Yeah? And who the fuck are you?"

The man willing to lay down life and limb for Dove's best friend.

I drop my voice to level with him. Man-to-man. "As

someone who has made his fair share of mistakes, I recommend you stop while you're ahead."

It takes the steam out of his pot, at least. He sucks his teeth, turns away, and goes back to the bar.

Crisis de-escalated, I go back outside, into the cold.

Ophelia is surrounded by her friends. She closes her eyes and groans, swaying on her feet.

"Want me to kill him?" Carver asks.

"We'll make it look like an accident," Princess agrees.

"I'm going to be sick." Ophelia shivers.

Phantom approaches her. "Ophelia," he says gently. "I'm—"

"Red," she says suddenly.

Phantom looks slapped. At her safe word, he immediately stops in his tracks, as though he's hit a glass wall. He takes a quiet step back. Giving her space.

Ophelia's birthday is ruined. Party's over.

Ophelia tucks into Dove and turns away from her friends.

"Just take me home," she begs. "I want to go home."

"I know, baby," Dove murmurs. She holds the other woman tight.

Phantom has moved away from the girls. He's on the sidewalk, eyes scanning the road for a cab. I join in beside him.

"I just don't get it," I say. "He spent all that time creating the scavenger hunt for her, and then he doesn't give a shit at all."

Phantom gives me a look like I've lost the plot.

"Brody didn't make the scavenger hunt."

If Brody didn't, then who…?

Ah.

It makes sense now, Phantom's lack of participation in the hunt. He wasn't bored. He just knew where the clues were the whole time.

His gaze finds the road again. It's started to snow again. It clings to his hair, dusting his shoulders. "Do you love Dove?"

I want to tell him something else. But he's told me his truth. In a stupid, uncharacteristic moment of honesty, I say: "Yes."

He doesn't hold it against me. He just nods solemnly.

"City magic, right?" he says.

He holds out his arm. A yellow cab comes as though summoned and pulls up beside us.

"Make sure they get home safe," Phantom says. Then he steps away.

The girls stumble over. Dove eases Ophelia inside the cab. She gives Princess a tight hug, then climbs in the cab herself.

I linger. Should I stay? Go?

What does Dove want?

The night's taken a turn.

"Dorian!" Dove leans out the cab and motions me in. "You coming?"

Of course.

I get in the cab and close the door behind me. The car jerks forward. Ophelia is bent over her knees, groaning, as Dove rubs her back. I glance back through the window. It's started snowing again, and it clings to the window, erasing the Seekers from view.

* * *

Ophelia gets sick in the cab.

Then again outside their apartment building as Dove struggles to get the keys in the door.

Ophelia and Dove live on the third floor of a walk-up. It takes us twice as long to get upstairs as I half-carry Ophelia under my arm, doing my best to keep her upright.

As we tumble into their apartment, Ophelia makes a choking sound. "Bathroom?" I ask urgently.

"Over there," Dove points to a closed door and I immediately steer Ophelia towards it. I get her inside and she stumbles to the toilet, barely making it there before she throws up again. I crouch behind her, quickly pulling her thick hair back from her face.

"*Fuck!*" she spits into the toilet.

"You're alright," I tell her.

"I'll get you some water," Dove says, lingering in the doorway.

"And crackers," I add. "Something salty."

Dove vanishes. I continue to hold Ophelia's hair and rest my hand on her back, feeling her body arch and shiver as she gets sick. It's unpleasant, but I feel nothing but pain for Ophelia as she voids herself of the night—the alcohol, the partying, and the grief. Dove returns, and between the two of us, we manage to get Ophelia to drink water and nibble on a few saltines.

Dove starts the shower. My cue to exit.

"Make yourself at home," Dove says over her shoulder. "Whatever!"

I leave the girls to it and close the bathroom door behind me.

In the brief silence, I give myself a moment to take stock of my surroundings.

I am in Dove's apartment.

It feels strangely sacred, like entering a temple. The apartment is small—typical of city apartments. There's a kitchen that joins a…*whatever* room, I suppose. A couple of beat up couches, a TV, and a window crisscrossed with a fire escape, overlooking the street. To the right is the bathroom and two closed doors—presumably, Dove and Ophelia's bedrooms. The apartment is swathed in rich sepia tones

—oranges and reds and yellows. Brown bookcases over-stuffed with books, a beaten, patterned rug under the small coffee table. There's a painting on the wall and I take a moment to stare at it. It's—literally—*on the wall*, painted onto the open brick. It's a painting of a woman lying on her side, dreaming. Her hair tumbles down and down, until it's caught by a monster with long fingers and wild eyes. The monster swallows her hair, as though devouring her dreams.

As I stare at the picture, I notice I'm not alone. Someone is breathing, loudly. I glance down to see a French bulldog at my feet. It's as wide as it is long and it looks up at me with this crazed, loopy smile. Each breath sounds like an asthmatic old woman.

"Hello," I say. It pants at me.

I crouch down and rub my thumb and forefinger together. I give the animal a *tsk-tsk* sound. I'm a cat person—not a dog person—but it seems to work all the same. The dog pushes its flat, lumpy snout against the back of my hand. After a couple sniffs, it starts licking, these long, wet kisses.

Disgusting.

I love it.

The bathroom door clicks. I glance up to see Dove back in the room with me.

"I see you've met Spud," she says.

"Spud. Aptly named."

I straighten back up. She steps close to me. She pulls her fingers through my jacket. "Shit—she nailed you."

I was, unfortunately, in the splash zone. "It's fine," I tell her.

"Take it off. I'll throw it in the wash."

Her tone doesn't leave room for argument. I remove my jacket and shirt. They have a washer and drier stacked next to the kitchen, and Dove opens the washer, tosses my shirt in, and then struggles out of her own clothes. Now, she's in nothing but cute, black panties and a small, dark bra.

She bends over, tossing everything in the wash. She has a perfect body—supple in all the right places. Blood vessel tighten. My heart picks up a beat.

Dove crosses the room and goes into her bedroom. She leaves the door slightly ajar and I can't help but sneak a look in. It's dim, but I can make out the chaos of Dove's life—clothes, books, half-finished craft projects—all scattered about her tiny space.

"Can I help?" I ask.

A ball of fabric comes sailing out of her bedroom, straight at me. I catch it. "You can put that on," she says.

I unfold it. It's a fleece sweater with the word HARVARD across the front. Men's size.

"An ex-boyfriend's?" I ask. There's no hiding the sting of jealous in my voice.

"My brother's. He never went, he just thinks he's clever."

She exits the bedroom. She's pulled on a long t-shirt and a pair of tiny shorts.

She may as well be wearing top-of-the-line lingerie, the way by body responds to her. I'm worse than Spud, panting in the corner. *Settle down, boy.*

I pull on the sweater. It smells of frat boy and, faintly, of Dove.

Dove re-enters the bathroom with a, "hey, me again…" She transfers Ophelia from the bathroom to her bedroom. She comes back with Ophelia's soiled dress. She throws it all in the wash and the machine rolls and thumps to life.

She stands then and pushes her hair back from her face. The fun from the night has left her, and she looks tired now. Too sober. Worried about her friend.

I want to take it all away from her.

"Thanks for helping," she says. "Seriously. It makes a man

with an iron stomach to clean up the vomit of a woman he barely knows."

"She means a lot to you, so she means a lot to me."

Dove stares at me like I'm a puzzle she's trying to piece together. I see her considering her next move, and then she asks: "Do you want something to drink?"

"No."

Those green eyes look up at me. "What *do* you want?"

"I want to take over your kitchen."

* * *

I make us a 2 am dinner. She has a round, cheap table in the kitchen with two bright orange chairs. I set the plates down on the table and Dove lights up when she sees what's on the menu. Grilled cheese sandwiches with a huge heaping of pickles on her plate.

"Extra crispy, extra pickles," I tell her.

"You're a good listener," she says. She's all smiles, pleased.

"Only the important things."

Or: any time Dove opens her mouth.

I sit across from her and we both dig in. My stomach pinches at the smell of cheese on toasted bread. This is exactly what my body needs right now, and I wolf down half of the sandwich.

Dove lifts a half, gesticulating. "If I could live off of one cheese the rest of my life, it would be gruyere. Underrated. Well, no. Maybe cheddar. I know that's a basic answer, but it's so good."

"Nothing wrong with basic." I could listen to her talk about cheese for days.

Her eyes connect with mine. Those emeralds glitter. With food in our bellies, we've both woken up. "Tonight was… pretty insane."

"In a good way or a bad way?"

She scrunches her face. She's fucking adorable. "Both?"

My eyes drift. There walls are covered with vibrant images—portraits of women with cartoonish creatures crawling all over them. "I like your wallpaper."

A light blush tinges her cheeks. "Oh—yeah. Those are my scribbles."

"You did those?"

"Yeah…I…I don't know. It's weird. I started painting on the walls and kinda couldn't stop. Ophelia likes it, which is good. I went on this kick of woman vs. monster. I liked the idea of creating visual images of these fears and anxieties we have constantly looming over our shoulders…these nagging voices in our head. *You're too old, you should smile more, your dreams don't matter.* Our everyday monsters."

"It's powerful."

"Thanks." She stares at her work, her eyes unfocused. "I've had a hard time working on canvases ever since the breakup. I needed…I don't know…"

"A canvas that could take a beating."

A half-grin slides up her mouth. "Yeah. Exactly."

Silence drifts between us. Not uncomfortable. Soft, thoughtful silence.

She's opened the door, so I walk through it. I ask her, "How did you feel about seeing Shawn tonight?"

Her chewing slows. I can see the wheels in her brain turning as she contemplates her answer. "It was…strange. I don't think I've processed it completely, to be honest."

"Do you want to talk about it? Why you two broke up."

She stops chewing completely. She wipes her hands on her napkin and I see resolve stitch its way into her features. "It was at Ophelia's party, ironically. He gave me an ultimatum. Him or The Seekers Club."

"And you chose the club?"

"No. I chose him. I just wanted to give him what he want-ed." Her eyes go unfocused. She's staring at a spot on the wall, but I can tell she's somewhere else. Back there. Back *with him.* "We went home that night and he...we got in bed. The mood was just...tense. He put his hands around my neck. He kept saying, *This is what you want, isn't it?* And like, yes, but not like that. He was so angry and I...I got so scared..."

A small whimper leaves her. Her hand flies to her mouth as though to keep it in check. But suddenly her face goes red and eyes fill with tears. They spill down the curve of her cheek.

"Oh, God," her voice trembles. "Sorry. I don't know what's happening."

My heart breaks.

I get up from my chair and go over to her. I kneel down in front of her, lowering myself to look up at her. I drop my voice. "Can I hold you?"

She nods. Her voice is small when she says: "Please."

I pull her chair back. I scoop her up, sit down, and take her in my lap. I wrap my arms around her and she cradles herself against me. Her hair is soft against my nose as she buries her face into my chest. She smells like fruity shampoo.

She shudders. It's a full-body shiver with a small twitch, like a hiccup in her system. The sweater gets damp with her tears. I hold her tight.

She confesses, "I don't think I've felt safe...for a very long time..."

"You're safe here," I tell her. "You're safe with me."

She cries. These don't feel like sad tears. They feel like a release. Like the sobs that come after a rough scene. That cathartic, therapeutic crying.

This is aftercare, a year too late.

I rock her soft weight in my lap. I hold her until she's let it all out and her tears are reduced to small, occasional sniffles.

"Thank you," she murmurs, "for being there tonight."

I'll be there every night.

I'll be there for the rest of your life.

I don't say that, though. Instead I reach for her plate. "Pickle?"

She nods. She tilts her chin up and I hand feed her. She takes a bite and crunches softly. I can feel her jaw working against my chest. Even the sound of her tiny crunches gives me peace. Her weight seems to get heavier as she relaxes into me. She lets out a small, soft sigh, as though relieved that she can finally hang this night up.

I drop my arm around the small of her back. I draw my thumb back and forth across the small of her back. I hold her up, anchoring her. Stabilizing her.

For a moment, we just linger in this soft, quiet intimacy.

"God," she sighs. "What a night."

"What a night."

The warmth of her breath hits the side of my neck. She tilts her head, and we're so close like this. Her gaze falls to my mouth. My heart is pounding like the rapid fire click of typewriter keys against my chest. She tilts forward, but then—

"Dove?"

There's Ophelia's voice, soft and sick from the bedroom.

Dove pulls away. "I should…"

"Of course."

I loosen my hold. She climbs out of my lap and gets up, vanishing back in Ophelia's bedroom.

Spud sits across from me, mouth open, like he's laughing. His heavy breaths rattle in time with the radiator. I rip him off an edge of cheesy bread and he takes it in a single swallow. I don't think he even chews. I'm his new best friend.

I clean our plates. Moments later, Dove exits the bedroom. There's an apology in her eyes. "I think I need to be with her."

I dry my hands. "I'll get a cab."

Relief in her eyes. She's too tired to put up a fight.

Dove walks me out of her apartment. We linger in the hall, and I tug on the sweater. "I'll return this."

"I have one of yours. You have one of mine. We're even." She folds her arms across her chest, leaning back against the door.

It's chilly in the hall. Her nipples are hard underneath her shirt, and her shorts are too short around those bare legs. I'm getting bad ideas. *I need to go.*

"Thanks again," she says. "For—"

"Don't ever thank me." My tone is firm. "You need me. I'm here. I had a good night."

Her eyes crinkle, amused. "Yeah. Me too, actually."

Her eyes linger on me. I feel exposed, suddenly, the way she's looking at me, as though she can see through my clothes, through my skin and muscles, to the blood pumping too quickly through my veins. She reaches out, her fingers tracing across my chest.

"You're a good man, Dorian," she says decisively.

A good *man*. Not a good boy. Not a good pup.

A good man.

My throat goes unexpectedly tight. I can't explain how healing it is to hear those words out loud, after years of being called things like *bad boy, homewrecker, disappointment.*

"Goodnight, Dove," I tell her.

"Night."

I lean in. I press a small, sweet kiss to her lips. Simple. Chaste. Innocent.

A *goodnight* kiss.

Then I pull away.

Go, I tell my feet. *Move.*

But Dove's green-eyed stare roots me in my place. Everything in me feels hyper-focused. I can see every freckle dotting her cheeks. The flutter of every eyelash. The way her plush lips fall open, just a little, as she sucks in a tight, shaky breath.

Dove reaches for me. She grips the sweater, yanks me against her, and pushes her lips heatedly against mine.

Fuck it. I unlock.

I dive my tongue into her mouth. I kiss her the way I want—the way I've been craving all night. No. *All year.* For months on end. I claim every inch of her mouth, devouring her, mapping her. I crush her body against the wall and I feel her hips press back, wanting. My tongue lashes against hers and she moans into my mouth, her body giving a small, tight buck against mine.

I plant my palms on her doorframe. I imagine there are chains on my wrists, hooking them to the wall. I have to keep my palms on the wall. If I move my hands to her body, it'll be all over. I won't be able to stop touching her. I'll fuck her, right here, in the hallway, not giving a single damn about who might walk in on us. I'll make her scream until she wakes the entire building. I won't stop, not until I have her clenching around my cock.

I'll be back to making no good, terrible choices, and I can't have that.

Dove deserves better.

Dove deserves everything.

She swallows my tongue, licking me back. Sucking. My self-control strains. I dig my fingers into the wall until I feel paint chips bite into my nailbed.

I break our kiss. I have to. Our lips are wet and we're both gasping for breath.

"You'll come back later?" she says. "To drop off the…um…"

"Sweater."

"Right. Sweater."

"Yes. I promise."

I risk another small, dangerous kiss that leaves us both shuddering. I unlatch my hands from the wall and peel myself away from her.

It's the hardest thing I have to do, but it's the right thing to do.

Tonight's not the night.

"Goodnight," I say again. Meaning it this time.

She smiles, and fuck, my heart does a full flip in my chest. "Get out of here."

Dove goes inside and closes her door, vanishing behind it.

1 4

LOVE FUCKING SUCKS

DOVE. **Now.**

My heart is racing a million miles a minute.

That kiss felt better than most *fucks*. I'm spinning, light-headed, when I go back inside my apartment.

What in the name of Christmas insanity is happening?

My hand trembles when I reach for my wine glass. I knock the rest of it back in one go, hoping the wine will steady me. And maybe distract me from the wet, messy puddle I've made in my panties.

Straight to the naughty list this year, Dove. Nothing but coal for you.

I take in a deep breath and exhale. Now is not the time to ride the horny train. I need to be there for Ophelia, who is still heartbroken and mourning the death of her birthday.

Snap out of it. Back into friend mode.

I knock gently on Ophelia's door and open up. "You still breathing?"

She's underneath a pile of thick, dark comforters. She's

wrapped the blankets around her like a nest, and I only know she's alive because I hear her answer from under the blankets: "Unfortunately."

I climb into bed with her. I get under her blanket castle and, wordlessly, we wrap around each other. She's sweaty and slick but *I don't care*. She's my best friend. The other half of my heart. And right now, hers is breaking.

She rests her head on my chest. "You were right," she says. "Love fucking sucks."

"Yeah," I agree, "it's a real bitch."

Slowly, Ophelia's breathing changes to a slow, quiet rumble. I stare at the ceiling, still tasting Dorian on my lips, and my heart flutters around like a million pillow-freed feathers dancing in my chest.

15

—————

ANOTHER LIFE

Dove. Then.

"The freaks or me. Make your choice."

Shawn stands there, his ultimatum like a sword in my chest.

Everyone at the club is watching me. Waiting to see what I'll do.

I stand. I feel outside of my body as I watch myself rise and go to stand next to Shawn.

He grins. That smug, self-satisfied smirk. "Good girl. Let's go home."

He turns and quickly walks down the hallway, out of the club. I follow behind him. My skin feels numb, like plastic wrapped around my bones.

"Yeah, get the fuck out of here!" Ophelia snaps to our retreating forms. "No one wants you here anyway!"

She's talking to Shawn. I know she's talking to him. But she's talking to *me*, too.

My eyes sting with tears. Shawn is walking too quickly,

190

already out the door, and I'm tripping over myself to try to keep up with him. My vision blurs, barely holding onto the tears, and as I exit the brownstone, I trip over the stone steps.

I brace for impact, but a strong hand catches me.

"Watch yourself," my rescuer says. His voice is heavy. Stern.

Familiar.

I look up at him, and I remember.

It's Dorian. Dorian from a year ago. The same blue eyes and dark hair, but perhaps a little more hectic around the edges. His hair is a little longer. The beard a little scruffier. There's a sleepless darkness circling his eyes.

He's raw as a nerve, and I can see it in the crease of his mouth. That frown I know so well is sharper, angrier.

There's a woman waiting for him at the top of the steps. Despite the cold, she's wearing a short, thin dress that shows off her long legs.

"Poe!" Quinn says. "Come on!"

Her voice pitches with impatience. Impatience and a hint of something else, too. We are staring at each other a bit too long.

This is a real memory, isn't it?

I'd erased bits and pieces of that night, my brain trying to protect itself. But I remember now. That's why he'd seemed familiar on the app—we ran into each other on that night. That night he took her up to the top floor and did things that made him hate himself the next morning. That night I went home with Shawn and he put bruises around my throat.

On the worst night of my life, I met my soulmate for the first time.

I just wasn't ready for him yet.

And he wasn't ready for me, either.

He's still holding onto me, his grip tight on my arm. I can't stop staring at him. Snow is falling gently around us and a snowflake traps itself in his dark eyelashes. Something flickers in his eyes—like perhaps his soul recognizes mine, too.

His eyebrows scrunch together. He must read my expression, because concern touches his face. "Are you alright?"

This is a dream. I can do whatever the hell I want.

In this version of the memory, I make a different choice. I grab Dorian and I kiss him.

He goes stiff at first, but then he de-thaws. His tongue melts in my mouth. I open for him, inviting, and he goes deeper. His hand curls around the small of my back, pulling my body flush against his, and a moan escapes me and bleeds into him.

Quinn is shouting for Dorian. Shawn is shouting at me. But neither of us pay any attention to them. Their voices are muffled by the sounds of our breaths and our hearts, beating and pounding together.

I wrap my body around his. He cradles his arms under me, supporting me as I pull my legs around his hips. Our lips never once break contact, our kiss only getting deeper, more heated. I reach between us and free him from his pants.

When he pushes inside of me, it's a fullness that heals something empty inside of me. I cry out against his mouth. He moans my name, and with that first burst of pleasure, I explode into a million tiny feathers.

16

CHRISTMAS DAY

DOVE. **Now.**

I jerk awake. My heart is pounding. The small of my back is slick, sticking to the sheets. My panties are soaked, too, the fabric clinging to me. It takes me a second to reorient; the walls are different. That's when I remember: I'm not in my own bed. I'm in Ophelia's bed. The whole room is warm and cozy, the radiator working double-time. The blankets are twisted up, but there's no Ophelia. Instead, when I roll over, I come face to face with Spud curled up in a ball on the pillow.

"Morning, cuddle bud," I tell him.

He opens his mouth in a droopy-tongue smile. He farts.

I groan. "Gross."

Okay, well. Guess I'm up.

I check my phone. A couple *Merry Christmases* in the family group chat. A second notification from the Seekers Club app.

THE SEEKERS CLUB

Happy holidays. If you'd like to spend some time with non-biological family, you're welcome here. Our home is your home. Doors open at 7.

I can't help it—I get a little choked at that. *It does feel good to be back home.*

The wooden floors are cold under my feet. My muscles ache from running around the city all night and I have delicious bruises on my knees from *that moment* with Dorian in his bookstore. I leave Ophelia's bedroom and I'm greeted with the smell of coffee.

A chilled breeze swoops through the room. The window is cracked open and Ophelia is sitting on the fire escape. It's snowed overnight, and she's sitting in a small pile of snow, jacket swallowing her, coffee in hand.

The coffee pot is still brewing—bless Ophelia. I make myself a mug, then pull on a sweater and don my pigeon beanie. I lift the window and Ophelia slides her legs up so I can take my spot sitting across from her.

"Merry Christmas," I tell her.

She tilts her mug towards me. "Merry fucking Christmas."

Her eyes look puffy and tired. We clink mugs. It's freezing out here, the cold biting my cheeks and eating at my fingers, but the coffee warms my hands and throat, sliding through my chest and stomach.

For a minute, we nurse our hangovers and savor the liquid gold caffeine.

"You know what's annoying?" she says.

"Tell me."

"Here I am, thinking, aw, what a sweet guy. He's gone through all this work to give me a scavenger hunt to solve on my birthday because he knows I love puzzles, right? And then—no, just kidding. He just wanted me out of his hair for five hours so he could make out with some woman in a tiger suit."

I sigh. "What is it about the tiger suit?"

"I would've worn a tiger suit. I would've worn a whole furry costume if that's what gets him off."

"I know, babe. You fell in love with the wrong person. That's not your fault."

"No?"

"City magic. Remember?"

Ophelia sighs. "Is this our new tradition? Every year, one of us gets our heart broken. We'll just keep going back and forth, over and over, until we give up and create a lesbian commune?"

I cock my head. "I'll be your wife."

"I'll be yours." A smile climbs up her lips. "Hey…up until Brody? That might've been the best night of my life."

Screw sugarplum fairies—memories of "shot-skis," public pillow fights, and Dorian's low-throated moans dance in my head. "Mine too." I knock my leg against hers. "What do you want to do today? It's your day. We'll do whatever you want."

She looks at me. "Did you get the Seekers Club notification?"

I nod. "I did."

She presses her lips together. "I want to go to the club and get spanked until I cry. Big, hard, life-ending cries."

I get it. I do. What we do at the club, the lifestyle—it's more than sex. It's more than deviancy. Sometimes, it's release. Permission to let go. Permission to scream.

I make a decision. It's time to break my hiatus. "I'll come with you."

She blinks, surprise showing over her expression. "Yeah?"

"Yeah."

A smile—a real smile—draws across her mouth. "I love you. You know that, right?"

"Love you more."

We savor our coffees as new flurries start to fall, clinging to our jackets and melting on our skin.

* * *

But first—I have a shift at Cheese Louise.

Normally, I might be peeved about working on Christmas day. But today, I've got a renewed pep in my step. Besides, it's only a half-day shift, and Louise and Marvin gave me a generous bonus for doing it. I don't even mind the rush of people, people who had last-minute change of plans, people who realized that they actually need to feed their guests Christmas morning, and that oh-shit customer who woke up Christmas day and realized he forgot to buy his wife a gift. The day keeps me busy, talking to customers, packing up orders. When there's a lull in the customers, I open up my phone and check my messages in the Seekers' Club App. There's a new message from Dorian.

DORIAN

How's the patient?

ME

She's on the mend.

Good to hear. I owe you a sweater.

"Sweater" I'm pretty sure is officially our code word for "a hard, all-night fuck-fest." At least, I hope it is. My thumb hovers over the screen and I type out my next words.

ME

I'm going to the club tonight.

The bubble pops up. He's typing. Then it vanishes. Finally, he sends:

DORIAN

Have fun.

I frown at his response. Last night was different. Authentic. *Real.*

So why does it feel like he's closing off again?

Did he wake up to a new, bright-white day, with a clear head and decided to forget all about the kiss we shared in the hallway?

Stop. No. Don't catastrophize.

The more reasonable, logically explanation: just because you're ready to go back to the club, *doesn't mean he is.* That place was a home for both of us…but it was also where some of our more traumatic nights happened.

I can't take it personally if he's not up for it.

I try to push my doubts aside. I'm locking up the teller when the chime rings above the door.

"Sorry," I say, "we're closing up—"

But I recognize the person who's come in, and my words die on my tongue.

Gingers offers a timid, half-smile. "Sorry," she says. "I was, um. I was just hoping to catch you for a couple minutes."

She's wearing a large jacket with furred edges. It swallows her. Her hair is tied back in a ponytail. She is as she was last night—stunning, put together.

Except for one, noticeable difference.

She's removed the black-and-pink collar from her throat.

"Soft or hard?" I ask.

She blinks. "Sorry?"

"Cheese. Which do you prefer?" I wave a hand. "Fuck it. I'll just make us a sample plate. Turn that sign to *Closed,* will you?"

* * *

We close up the shop and talk and snack on cheese for nearly an hour.

Or rather, Ginger talks. I let her vent.

Her story is all too familiar. One I know painfully well. But there's a key difference that gives me hope: she left before it went from bad to *terrible*.

I give her positive reinforcement. I give her my number. And I introduce her to the Seekers Club app. "It's open tonight," I tell her. "You don't have to come. But I'll be there, if you want a friendly face."

"Thanks." She looks hesitant about accepting it, but at least she looks lighter than when she came in.

We share a hug. I wrap up a package of sheep's milk cheese that she devoured and send her off with it. Then I *officially* close up shop and head back to the apartment.

I've got a couple hours before we have to head to the club. Ophelia's door is closed, music blaring. She's shaking off last night and hyping herself up.

I realize I've left last night's clothes—including Dorian's jacket—in the wash. I quickly transfer them to the dryer. When I do, something heavy falls out onto the floor.

It's a set of keys. Can't be Dorian's apartment—he got home somehow, right? I remember him pulling them out last night. They have to be the set to his bookstore.

And, in that moment, I get an idea.

Probably a bad one.

But you only get one lifetime, right?

I snatch up the keys, pack a bag, and Spud gives me a disapproving *woof* as I head back out.

WE'RE INSANE PEOPLE

Dorian. **Now.**

Morning breaks. I am depleted.

I wake up to Behemoth making biscuits on my chest, his needle claws leaving pinpricks on my skin. My head is pounding. At thirty-six, I am too fucking old for tequila shots, this hangover is going to level me for the next two days, how the hell did I let Ophelia talk me into that, I should've been in bed by 9 pm, and—

I am so fucking happy.

Dove kissed me. Me. My lips. On her mouth. In her hallway.

My body? Broken. My head? Decimated. My heart? Full. So full.

I give Behemoth his Christmas present (a catnip toy that makes him lose his mind), and go through my notifications. Maggie sent pictures of Christmas morning. There's one of my nieces—four and six—pretending to be secrets agents with their new nerf guns, standing back to back in their PJs.

I can't help but chuckle.

My nieces are hilarious curated in their matching pajama outfits, but they have untamed eyes and wild smiles that give me hope for the next generation. I keep scrolling and come to a full family photo—my sister, our parents, and Mark and Quinn.

Her image used to be a punch in the chest. But now?

She looks like a stranger. Like a character from someone else's story.

This is a good, healthy feeling. Healthier than I've felt in a long time.

But I should know better. Happiness is always brief and fleeting.

Because as soon as I get comfortable (a cup of coffee, a book, and an exhausted and high cat in my lap), chaos erupts. A loud, pitchy alarm from downstairs. It's the bookstore. Someone is breaking into my bookstore.

Mother*fucker*...

Who robs a bookstore on Christmas day? I leap out of my sitting nook and Behemoth tumbles out of my lap and onto his paws with an irritated yowl. I go into my closet, where a baseball bat sits behind my winter jackets solely for this purpose. I grab it by the neck and exit my apartment. I skip the elevator, flying down the stairs instead. If this is Santa, I'm going to break his nose.

My phone buzzes at my hip when I reach the bottom. I answer it.

"Ironlock Security," says a voice on the other end. "Is this Dorian Lennon? We've received a notification that your location has been broken into."

"Yeah. I know." I exit the apartment complex. It's a disarmingly bright day.

The glass on the windows and door is un-shattered. I touch my doorknob. It's unlocked. What the hell?

"Would you like us to send the police?"

"Not yet. I'm going to check it out."

"John Cena?"

"What?"

"Are you the legendary wrestler John Cena? Because otherwise, I would advise against it."

"Fuck you," I tell him. Which is—admittedly—perhaps a little strong for Christmas. "Just stay on the line. I'll let you know what I run into."

"Sir, I would really advise against it."

I put my hand on the door and—for a second—I pause.

Hold on.

I'm running into the bookstore. With a bat. Am I really ready to beat someone to death for absconding with a copy of *Pride and Prejudice*?

No. Well. Maybe my Spanish copy of *Tender is the Flesh*. That might deserve the death.

I suck in a breath. Do or die, Dorian.

I still have my reading glasses on my face. I adjust them, twist the handle, and burst into the bookstore. There he is. The thief. Silhouetted in the kids corner.

My heart is kicking like a wild animal in my chest.

"Hey!" I shout, mustering up as much masculine aggression as I can throw into my voice. Bat in one hand. Phone in the other.

He screams. No—wait. *She* screams.

Dove jumps around, wide-eyed. She sees the bat and freezes in place. The paint can in her hand drops to the floor with a heavy thud. She's wearing overalls, like a sexy Bob Ross.

"Hello?" The operator says. "You dead, John Cena?"

Dove has an *oops?* expression written all over her face.

I feel my teeth grind. I exhale a slow, thin breath. "False

alarm," I tell him. I put down the bat and lean it against a bookshelf. "It's my fucking girlfriend."

"Copy that. So I can deactivate the alarm?"

"Please. Happy holidays."

Then I end the call. The second I do, the blaring alarm cuts off.

For a second, Dove and I stand there in the deafening silence.

She points to my phone. "Did you just call me your girlfriend? I feel like we should unpack that."

My adrenaline is pounding too fast to metabolize her cuteness. "What are you doing here?"

She lifts her palm. My key ring dangles from her pointer finger. "You left your keys. I just thought—"

"You just thought you'd *break in?* And—what." I motion to the paint can. "Redecorate? Are you insane?"

Even I'm aware there's a heat in my voice I need to tame. But Dove doesn't back down. Instead, her lips thin. She crosses her arms and cocks her hip. "Yes. I am. And it's your fault."

I bark a laugh. "*My* fault?"

"Yes. You. You have me acting in ways that are uncharacteristic. Frankly, alarming." She motions to the wall. "I was going to repaint your stupid owl. It was supposed to be a grand, romantic gesture!"

Now, she's yelling at me. Guilt dissolves on my tongue and softens my tone. "You hate grand, romantic gestures."

Her mouth pinches in a frown. "Yeah, but since you've got a cast-iron heart that can't take a hint and recognize that someone might, god forbid, care about you, I've resorted to breaking and entering to spell it out in big, brush-shaped letters."

We're squared off now, two bulls caught in each other's horns. Dove isn't an intruder—she's something far more threatening to my sanity—and my heart hasn't slowed down since I burst through that door.

"I didn't ask for this," I hear myself say. A weak protest.

Her laugh is bitter. "You didn't ask for this? Hell, *I* didn't ask for this. You think I wanted to fall in love with a reclusive, self-loathing, bratty submissive?"

Fall in…

Love?

Did she say love?

She doesn't say the word that way I say the word. Loaded with shame. She says it with her full chest. Her eyes on mine. Bold. Vulnerable.

Braver that I could ever be.

The words I want to say back twist into a tight knot around my vocal chords.

Instead, I step forward, closing the gap between us.

She has to tilt her head up now to keep her eyes on mine.

"That's not entirely true," I tell her. I slide my hand gently across the side of her face. The warmth of her cheek touches my palm. I keep going, travelling through her hair. When I get to the back of her neck, I pull her into a tight grip and correct her: "I'm a self-loathing, bratty *switch*."

At the strength of my grip, her lips part, breath going light. Her eyelids flutter, and when those green eyes meet mine again…

There she is.

My Dove.

My good girl.

No—not girl.

Bad. Very bad.

Bad. And devious. And fucked up in all the ways I'm fucked up.

I've never wanted a person more in my entire life.

She launches herself at me. We clash clumsily, her lips

bruising mine in her haste, my glasses tilting on my nose. I cup her cheek, thumb wedging underneath her jaw to stabilize her. Her fingers climb to the top of my head and she fists a handful of hair, pulling at my roots. It nearly cuts my legs out like marionette strings and I hear myself groan into her mouth.

This is our tug-of-war, isn't it?

Me, anchoring her.

Dove, unraveling me.

I don't break our kiss, but I pant against her mouth: "My bedroom's upstairs."

"I can't wait that long." She drops her hands to my jeans and unbuttons me. "I need you inside of me."

Yes. She does. And so do I.

I'm so hard, Michelangelo could use my dick to carve a sculpture of Dove out of marble. But even the Renaissance master couldn't capture the best parts of her. The way strands of her hair stick to her lips. The flair of her nostrils on that adorable, button nose. That untamable hunger in her eyes.

Dove is wearing overalls. *Overalls.* A goddamn chastity belt on a human and yet I am feral for her. I unpin the straps over her shoulders and push it down her body so she's in nothing but a shirt and panties. She yanks my shirt up over my head. Our mouths meet again and this time, I leave bruises on her lips with my need.

"Who's on top?" she mumbles against my mouth.

"Fuck if I know," I growl.

I take off her shirt and we sink to the floor. Which answers the question—currently, right now, I'm on top. My pants are undone, which relieves a little pressure, and with Dove on her back, I follow a trail down her body. I slide my hands down her sides. Her nipples are tight and hard and my mouth waters at the sight of them.

I want to take them in my mouth. I deny myself. I kiss between the curves of her breasts. I kiss her sweet stomach.

Her fingers lock into my hair and twist in a way that makes me twitch. When I look up at her, those green eyes are staring at me inquisitively. "Tell me what you want," she says.

I answer honestly. "I need to taste you."

She pushes her hips up towards me. Encouraging. "Fuck, I need that too."

She nudges my head down. But I stall her. I grabs her wrists and pin them to the floor on either side of her, trapping her underneath me.

Even I barely recognize my own voice for the heat in it when I tell her:

"Settle down, Dove. It's my turn to torture you."

18

FERAL ANIMALS

Dove. Now.

One second, we're kissing.

Not soft, sweet, intimate pecks, either.

Frantic, clothes ripping, lip biting, hungry kisses. He devours me the way a wolf devours a lamb, and I try to climb inside his mouth and make a home there.

The next thing I know, I'm down to my panties on the floors, hips arching, looking for some friction, *anything*, anything to ease this ache deep, deep inside of me.

Dorian eases down my body. He removes his reading glasses and sets them aside, getting down to business. His fingers curl around my panties, inching them down my hip, and his lips brush the bared skin there.

Those blue eyes meet mine. "Permission to—?"

"Yes." I pant. "Yes. To everything."

He rewards me with an affectionate bite, a little taste of pain that sends a shiver through me. He slides my panties down, rolling them off my legs. I part my legs. Begging. Wanting.

I watch Dorian as his eyes fall between my legs. He pinches my sex open, admiring me all while keeping his fingers away from the place I need him most.

"You're beautiful. You know that?" His head drops and his hair tickles my thigh. His large hand roves up my body, cupping one of my tits, and he squeezes, pinching my nipple between his thumb as he inhales me. My body twists—arching into his hand, towards his mouth.

"You smell so good, Dove," he murmurs. "I want to wear you like cologne."

He bites the skin on my thigh and I yelp in surprise. His hand moves to my other breast, kneading. I'm a livewire under him. Every part of my body he touches jolts to life, like he's waking me up, inch by inch.

His hand slides a slow path down my body. When it comes between my legs, he finally dips his fingers into my dripping core. He slides against my slippery slit and I mewl, too horny to be ashamed of the desperate noises coming out of my mouth at the mere hint of his touch. He parts my lips and the heat of his breath beats against my sensitive skin. "When was the last time someone worshipped this pussy the way it deserves, Dove?"

"I don't know."

He kisses me there. I feel the softness of his lips. The coarse hair of his short beard. When his tongue unfurls with a slow, hot caress, it sends a bolt of pleasure up my spine. I grip his hair and tug him against me, wanting more, but he takes both of my wrists and pins them to the carpet on either side of my body.

"No," he says. "This is for me. I'm going to enjoy you at my pace. Legs on my shoulders."

I obey. Happily. I move my legs over his shoulders. He shifts, lifting, and traps my wrists underneath my back, one of his hands clasping them in place. His other hand grips my thigh and his tongue gives a slow, hungry swirl around my clit that makes me hit the ceiling. I cry out as he sucks and licks. He's savoring me like I'm his favorite meal and every swipe of his tongue sends lashes of pleasure through me. With my hands pinned and my legs over his shoulders, I'm trapped, at the mercy of his devious tongue. My breath hitches and I feel myself squirming against his mouth, heels digging into the strong muscles of his back. My legs start to tremble uncontrollably as my pleasure pulls tight inside of me.

"Oh my God," I gasp. "I'm going to—"

"No, you're not." He pulls his mouth back. He releases my wrists from his grip and gives my thigh a quick smack. "Not yet. I'm going to make you explode on my cock."

His lips are shiny with me. He untangles my legs from his shoulders and sits up. My core aches, hanging on the edge. His hand slides between my legs and he slides a single finger inside of me. It rips a gasp from my lungs. He curls his finger and strokes my inner wall, making me tight with need. His eyes remain trained on me the entire time. "You want that, don't you? Say it."

"I want to come on your cock—*fuck!*"

His finger has me twisting with want. He dips his head back down and kisses me, returning his vicious onslaught to my clit. I try to obey—I try not to come—but I feel myself riding the edge with each stroke and lick.

I need to distract myself or I'm going to explode.

I wiggle a leg down his body. My foot finds his groin. I tease that hard bulge under his jeans, rubbing.

A puff of hot air hits my pussy. His hips jerk forward, rutting.

"Don't," he mumbles. There's that dark want in his voice that makes me flutter.

I nestle my foot against his length. "Mm. Don't what?"

"Don't be a bitch."

My hand moves to his face. I cup his cheek, yanking it up.

His lips are swollen and shiny. Those eyes are bright and vibrant. The second his eyes meet mine—I feel it. We've switched.

"What did you just say?" I ask. I push my thumb into his mouth. He lets me. I slide it against his rough teeth and that hard-working tongue.

He corrects himself: "Don't, *boss*."

I push my knee into his chest. He rolls onto his back and I flip on top of him. Perched on my knees, I lower myself back on his face. He grips my hips and nestles between my legs.

I slip my fingers through that thick, curly hair. His groan vibrates through me and makes me shiver.

"Stick out your tongue," I tell him, "and let me grind."

He flattens his tongue against my cunt and then goes still. I position myself so I can rub my swollen, achy clit against that sweet tongue.

"Good boy." I hear myself sigh. I tighten my fingers in his curls. "Good fucking boy."

The moans he makes is unholy. I know I'm playing with fire —teasing myself against his mouth—but I can't help it. It feels too good to stop. I ride the wave of my own pleasure, body clenching, clit throbbing against his tongue. I push myself to the very edge, my thighs quivering, tightening around his head.

But even there, there's the voice in my head—I'm not allowed to come like this.

And I better stop before I do.

"Take off your pants," I tell him, breathless.

He shifts underneath me. I slide off his face and shimmy

down his body, onto his lap. He sits up. He looks insane—lips and cheeks wet and shiny with me. His hair all askew from the way I'd been twisting it. His eyes have a lust-fueled film over them.

I dip down and catch his lips in mine. Our kiss is messy. He tastes like me. As I kiss him, I slide my hand down to that hard muscle. His cock is so stiff, it pulses in my hand. He groans in my mouth as I give him a couple languid strokes and guide him between my legs. I tuck his cock between my lips. But I don't take him inside. Instead, I grind against his hard length. I'm so wet, he's immediately slick with me. The friction makes the both of us shiver as I ride him, up and down, sliding myself over his length.

"You said I could come on your cock, right?" I ask.

"Yes, but—"

"Please." My voice is a sweet whine. I nestle against the side of his face. I kiss the edge of his mouth. "Can I please come on your cock?"

I rub myself over him. The muscle swells, throbs, drips onto his stomach.

He's not the only one who can be a brat. But, I mean, look at me. I'm fucking adorable. A sweet, needy little brat. The muscle in Dorian's jaw flexes. He's having a hard time saying *no* to me. He has a hard time denying me anything like this.

"Fuck," he swears. His voice is rough. "Bad girl."

I whimper. Each time I slide myself over his cock, it sends me inching closer and closer to the edge of relief. I'm desperate for it now—can a woman die from hanging on the edge for too long? It feels like I might. I lick up his neck. Nip his earlobe. And beg: "*Please*, sir."

He breaks. "Cum," he says. "Do it. Now."

A cry of relief escapes me. The second he gives me permission, my body takes it. My hips buck forward in tight little jerks. I cave forward, the orgasm too intense, but

Dorian grips my hair, using his strong grip to hold me up. I hear myself whimpering, I can hear little *oh gods*, and I drop myself into the crook of his neck. I inhale him—the smell of a leather-bound journal, well loved—and ride out my orgasm with desperate little mewls.

I'm reeling, twitching, my heart pounding. Dorian grounds me. He presses a single kiss right under my ear. There, his voice comes—that heavy, smooth tone. "You're so fucking horny, you couldn't wait."

I whimper. My voice doesn't work yet. That doesn't stop him from filling my ear with his filthy words: "Look at you," he continues darkly. "Pathetic. What a mess you've made on my cock."

Oh fuck.

"I should make you lick it clean."

Oh. *Fuck.* My cunt gives another tight squeeze at the thought.

"Do you want that?"

"Yes," I manage to get out.

"You love it when I use your mouth, don't you?" When I don't respond right away, he tightens his grip on my hair. Pain sparks over my skull, sending tingles all through my body. "Answer," he demands firmly.

"Yes, sir."

He hooks his hand on the back of my neck and starts to guide me down. "Eyes on me," he says.

I shift so I'm sitting on his thighs. I brace myself, my hands flat on the carpet on either side of his hips. Then, with my gaze fixed on his blue eyes, I slide my tongue out. I do a thorough job of cleaning him. First, I clean the thick pre-cum that's puddled in the creases of his abdomen. Then I travel my tongue over his full balls. Up his slick length. My gaze remains obediently on him as I trace over every inch, paying special attention to the places I know drive him crazy—the dark vein that climbs his length and that sensitive, blood-bruised, swollen head.

Never once do my eyes leave his face. I get to enjoy each shift in his expression. His throat bobs with a hard swallow. His jaw flexes. His pupils are blow. His fingers in my hair go tight, then lax, then tight again.

"Fuck, Dove." His voice is as coarse as steel wool. "I can't wait another second."

19

ENOUGH

Dorian. **Now.**

Enough.

Time to take what's mine.

I pull her up by the hair. Dove gives a small yelp, but she follows as I guide her over my desk. Fuck these books. I clean the space for her, shoving them to the floor, and sit her on the edge of the desk.

Those green eyes watch me. "How are you going to fuck me?" she asks. "Hard?"

I take her face in my hand. I rub my thumb over her soft cheek. "Yes."

"Are you going to leave bruises?"

"Yes."

"Do you want to come inside of me?"

My throat knots itself with want. I can barely croak out: "Yes."

"Do it." She nestles in close. We're both feral for each other—animals—but there's something intimate in her voice.

Something sweet that turns all my focus to her, like rope twisting tight. "Take me," she says. "Don't hold back. I want you to lose control. I trust you."

I trust you.

My world spins.

She's given me permission. Permission to lose control.

I trust you.

I lose it.

I spin Dove around. She gasps in surprise. I position her just how I want her. Her palms hit the desk. I push down on the back of her neck so she bends forwards, pushing her ass up towards me. I don't give her even a second to catch her bearings. I part her wet sex and sink myself inside of her.

My poor Dove. She's just come and her body is so tight. So tight, so wet, so *mine*. She cries out, her hips lifting from the desk, but I tell her, "You can take it."

And she does. Fuck. *She does.* I watch it slide inside of her. By the time I get it all the way to the hilt, her sweet little legs are trembling.

"Fuck," she whispers. "Fuck. You're so big."

I could come from this sight alone. I'm getting dangerously close.

I slide my hand up the back of her neck. I take a handful of her hair. I pull it aside and kiss her throat.

"Breathe for me," I tell her. She does and starts to relax around me. "You good?"

"Good," she says. She sounds delirious. "So fucking good."

All I need to hear.

I grip her hip and I take her. Hard. I push into her with the kind of rough passion that I've kept pent up for so long. The way I want her is hungry, and filthy, and Dove—

She loves it.

She cries out. Delicious, whimpery, *give me more* cries. I give her more. I give her everything I have. I fuck, and I grip, and I give until can't hold back anymore. I explode. It bursts from me and I hear this animal sound leave me—a dark growl from my throat—as I fuck her, filling her. Pleasure rushes from my toes, through my fingertips, down the center of me, pooling out from me and into her.

I hang over her, trying to catch my breath in the aftermath. Dove shudders underneath me—a beautifully spent angel.

She's the first to speak. "God," she moans. "That was so—"

I interrupt her. "I'm not done."

2 0

COME AGAIN?

Dove. **Now.**

I'm not done.

Every nerve in my body lights up when he says it. With excitement—and fear.

Can I handle more?

He slips out of me. He flips me around so I'm facing him, and I see the heat in those eyes, and I know—

Yes. I can handle it. More than that, I want this.

I want everything I have coming to me.

I deserve this.

I deserve every drop of this feral fucking man. My thighs are sore where they slammed over and over against the desk. Those red bands will turn purple and blue tomorrow, and I love them. I widen my legs. Inviting.

He pushes his cock back inside of me.

My head falls back. I moan, unable to stop my toes from curling as his thick length fills me once again. It's perfect, every goddamn inch of him. In one hand, he grips my thigh, holding me against him. In the other hand, he takes my throat. Pinning me to him. He holds me in a way that keeps me secure and my breath feels thinner, lighter, my head spinning as he pounds me.

In this position, my needy little nub grinds against the base of his cock. I whimper, the sound small and choked in his hand. I feel myself go tight, squeezing him, and I can't come again, I can't possibly come again, but here I am, pleasure cresting, bursting—

"*Dove!*" He shouts my name. He sounds almost pained, hips bucking violently against mine as we come together. We crash together—a throbbing, spilling mess. Two humans becoming one tangle of limbs and fluids and beating hearts.

I'm limp as a doll against him. If he wasn't holding me up, I'd be melted against the desk. Dorian has his head down, panting for breath. His skin is furnace hot against mine, the both of us are slick with sweat and *everything else.*

He still has his hand around my throat, that dominant hold, yet I'm the one who rasps: "Good boy."

He lifts his head. There's that wicked smile of his. He returns with, "Bad girl."

My heart flips in my chest. When he says it—it's not a punishment. It's praise. I'm *his* bad girl. It's what he loves most about me.

Bad is good. Top is bottom. Up is down and when his mouth meets mine, I can't help but whimper into his kiss.

"Can we do that again?" I ask. "And again and again?"

A laugh against my mouth. "You have to give me at least thirty seconds."

I trace my fingers over his chest and hum. "Twenty-nine..." I flick my finger over his hard nipple. "Twenty-eight..."

He growls. He takes my hand and wetly kisses my palm, nipping at the mound between my thumb and my wrist. It's not a *stop,* but he's right. We need to slow down before we combust.

"We have to stop fucking in my bookstore," he adds.

"Afraid of me leaving marks on your desk?"

"I'm afraid of you leaving marks on every aspect of my life."

The lust-haze is clearing. His eyes are blue and clear now when they meet mine. I move my hand to his chest. "Your heart is pounding."

I can feel him go tense to my touch.

He can handle my hand around his throat. Around his cock. But I put it against his chest, against his *heart,* and he still gets shy.

"Do you believe in kismet?" I ask him.

"Kismet?"

"Like…fate. Like maybe some people don't cross paths until they're meant to?"

A crooked smile from him. "Do you think we met in another life?"

"Sort of. I just…I had this dream. Well, more like a memory. I think we met last year. At the Seekers Club—"

"The night of Ophelia's party. Yes. I remember."

I blink. "You do?"

"Vaguely. I thought I was going crazy, until you said it."

"No. Not crazy. Not about this, anyway." His heart beat is slowing. We're in that dangerously vulnerable space after an amazing fuck-fest. Both of us, spilling secrets. Spilling truths. I ask him: "Do you wish you made a different choice that night?"

He lapses into a thoughtful silence. When he speaks, it's with confidence. "I don't know if I believe in fate. But I believe in you. And if I had to crawl through hell to get to this moment, right here…I'd do it a thousand times over. In a heartbeat." He strokes his thumb over my cheek, cradling my face. I feel so soft. So secure. "Whatever force brought me to you…fate, whatever you want to call it…I would like the opportunity to get to my knees and properly thank it one day."

A smile creeps up my lips. "That's the cheesiest thing you've ever said."

He nestles against me. The warmth of his breath hits my cheek. "You're turning me into gruyere."

I tilt my forehead against his. In this small, quiet space, I find myself making a confession, "Maybe you're gruyere. But I'm…curd."

"*Curd?*"

"Yeah. Immature cheese. Cheese that hasn't even begun the process of ripening."

"You've lost me."

"I'm…immature. Still figuring out who I am. What I want. I don't want you to fix me. I don't want to fix you. I don't want us to heal each other or make each other better people. I'm fucked up. You're fucked up. Let's just…be fucked up people together. We can hurt when we want to, and feel good when we want to, and—"

"Dove." I'm rambling, but my tongue cuts short when those sharp blue eyes meet mine. He tells me firmly: "You're perfect. Believe me when I say I wouldn't change a thing about you."

My throat gets tight. "Nothing?"

"Nothing. I love this version of you. And I'll love every version that comes after. I love you—every messy piece of you."

I love you. He said it! He said the words!

My heart might burst right out of my chest.

He drops his forehead against mine. I close my eyes. We breathe together, and I try to burn this exact moment into my memory.

Fuck. My cunt—and my heart—feel so full.

"Are you still going to the club tonight?" he asks.

"I was going to. But…"

"We should go. Together."

"You don't have to. It's…sort of a source of trauma. For both of us."

"Dove. *Do you want to go?*"

I bite my lip. Reminder to self: Dorian is and always will be a safe space to say the things I want out loud. So I answer honestly: "Yes."

Relief in his eyes. He nods. He presses a small, sweet kiss to my lips. The way you kiss someone when you've been married twenty years, and each kiss is muscle memory.

He says, "Then let's get dressed and go."

21

POE IS DEAD

Dorian. **Now.**

Eventually, Dove and I leave the bookstore. I take her to my apartment upstairs. The idea is to kill time before the club opens, but I would be remiss not to mention—

We fuck again in the shower.

And on my couch.

And (after a brief pause to wolf down some pizza) on the kitchen table.

It's official. My dick is made of fucking steel around Dove, and I can't keep the damn thing down when I'm in proximity of her.

Seven rolls around and it takes all my self-control just to get out the door. I chug a sports drink as Dove pulls her purse over her shoulders.

"What are you doing?" she asks.

"Replenishing." I hold it out for her. She shakes her head. "That wasn't a request."

She rolls her eyes, but she grinning when she puts the

bottle to her lips and takes a few lengthy swallows. I smack her on the ass. She chirps.

I could get used to this. All of it. Playing with Dove. Fucking Dove. The seamless way we switch. I feel like a man who has been sitting in a dark room for years and, suddenly, Dove flicked on a light.

She satisfies cravings I didn't know existed before.

We get downstairs and I whistle for a cab. Dove gets in first and I slide in beside her. As we settle in, I take her hand and lace my fingers through hers.

I can't keep my hands off of her.

She tilts her head against the seat. Her eyes are filled with this mirth that makes my heart flip in my chest. It's the feeling of being kids at a sleepover together—nothing but a fun night ahead of us.

"I can't believe I'm wearing overalls to the club."

"Does it matter? I'm ripping them off you the second we get inside." She twists her mouth at that. I back-peddle: "But we can stop at your place first. If you want."

"No, it's okay. It's…what do they call it? *Cozy kink?* I'm *literally* cozy kink."

"You look great."

"I look like I've just been fucked for four hours."

"That's what I said."

She bites on her lip. "When we go inside…are you going to be my dominant or my submissive?"

"I'll be whatever you want me to be."

"Mm. Sounds like a submissive answer."

"I'll be your dominant." *Don't tell me what to do.*

She looks amused by that. "Do you prefer one to the other?"

I shake my head. "What turns me on about being in a scene…it isn't necessarily dominating or submitting. Humiliating or being humiliated. What turns me on is that…for that hour, we're not on our phones or thinking about bills or replaying the worst moments in our lives over and over. I am solely, completely focused on you and you're focused on me. We're connected."

"Spoken like a true middle child."

"Do you have a preference?"

She shakes her head. "I used to. But…I like what we are. I like…feeling so protected one moment, and so powerful the next. It's fun, it's hot, and it's…healing. You give me space to do both."

"So do you."

"And I trust you to know what I need, when I need it. But…with that said, I think we need a word."

"Like a safe word?"

"Yeah. Or like a…*we're not speaking the same language, let's pause and check in* word."

I nod, slowly understanding. Things have shifted. We're negotiating again. It feels good to get on the same page. "What are you afraid of?"

"Like, what if I'm in sub-space and you start bratting? Or if you're dominant and then *I* go dominant and we kill each other?"

I tilt my head against the back of the seat. "I like the last one."

A grin teases her lips. "That's only because you know you'll lose."

Her fingers toy with mine. Fuck. I like fucking this woman. I like playing with her. I liked holding her hand. I even like *negotiating* with her. Just sitting here, in the back of a taxi, talking with her, is like a balm on my soul.

If my heart swells anymore, it might crack a rib.

"Kismet," I say.

"Kismet?"

"Yeah. *Kismet.* That's our safe word. It'll remind us that

even if we're out of sync in the moment…we'll find our way back to each other eventually."

I pull her hand to my lips and press a kiss to the back of her fingers.

She grins. "I love it."

But there's something bothering her still. I can tell. Something dancing in her eyes. For a moment, we sit in silence as people in puffy coats and snow-capped fire escapes pass us by.

Finally, Dove breaks the silence. "I have a…I don't know. A weird question."

"I have a weird answer."

"When we go inside, should I call you Poe?"

Even the mention of my old scene name makes my cheeks go hot with burning shame. I feel myself wince. "That name is dead. Just Dorian."

Relief crosses her expression, but I can tell she's trying to hide it. Instead, she just nods. "Okay."

"Or *sir*, if you're feeling frisky."

That makes her grin. "Yes, sir."

The cabbie is getting an earful, and is probably grateful when we make it to our destination. He slows to a stop on the familiar street. The unassuming brownstone is frosted with a coat of white. The reddish steps have been salted, but a layer of snow lines the pillars that outline the steps. The blinds are drawn, but there's a soft glow coming from inside.

The last time I was here, I was stumbling down those steps with that hollowed out, sick feeling of someone who had just royally fucked up the rest of his life.

The building is just a building. I remind myself of that, but I find myself gripping the handlebar all the same.

Dove's eyes flit over me. "Are you sure you're ready?"

She can read me like a book.

I crook my finger. "Kiss me, and then I'll answer."

She crawls over. She cradles my face in her hand and guides my face against hers.

Against her mouth, I mumble, "Now pull my hair."

As we kiss, her flingers slide into my curls. The scrape of her nails on my scalp send a shiver through me. Slowly, she takes a handful and grips tight. The sharp pricks of pain ground me, centering me back into my body.

It scratches an itch. The noise that escapes my throat is something like a purr.

Behemoth would be jealous.

Dove seals the kiss. "Well?"

"Yes. I'm ready."

She gives my bottom lip one last nip and then releases me from her grip, pulling away. My lips tingle in her absence. They miss her already.

I pay the cabbie and we get out. Dove reaches back, wiggling her fingers. I take her invitation and slide my hand on hers. Together, we climb the steps to the Seekers' Club.

I'm the first to pull out my phone. I check the updated code, then punch it into the keypad beside the door. The light blinks green and the door unlocks.

We enter, and the house embraces us in a warm hug.

The heat is blasting—makes sense, a lot of people here want to spend their time half-naked. Tonight, the ever-present scent of sex and longing is replaced by the crisp, clean smell of winter and pine tree. Phantom at least hasn't gone as far as to play Christmas carols (thank God), and the music plays low with a steady, sensual beat. The coat closet it open and I take Dove's coat off of her shoulders to hang it up.

Princess is sitting at her alcove near the door. She pops up when she sees us and grins. "Oh shit. It's you two."

"Trouble has arrived," I say.

"Happy holidays."

"Happy holidays, Princess."

She and Dove share a quick, tight hug. Princess pulls back to gestures to the tree. "We've got presents. Take something off the tree, yeah?"

The first floor is nicely decorated, with touches of Christmas lights, a menorah on the mantle, and a thick, healthy fir tree beside the fireplace. There are small presents tucked below and in the arms of the tree—some wrapped, others bare. All kinky—even from here, I can spot a pair of handcuffs, a bullwhip, and a strap-on harness.

We're not the first ones here. A few people are milling about. The fireplace is blazing. I spot Carver sitting on the stone beside it, talking to a woman in the armchair.

Dove lets out a happy shriek and rushes to the woman, arms in the air.

"Ginger! You came!"

The woman turns to us and—right. I recognize her now. Shawn's girlfriend from last night. I do a quick scan of the room, but no Shawn in sight.

Which is when I notice: her collar is missing from her throat. *Ah.*

"I came," Ginger says. "I just thought I'd...try something new."

She smiles. It's a shy smile. First-time jitters.

"She was admiring my nuts." Carver smirks. His sweater is stitched with an image of roasting chestnuts and the words: DEEZ NUTS ARE FIRE.

"Is Ophelia here?" Dove asks.

Carver lifts his eyebrows. "Can't you hear her?"

Then—we do. A loud cry from upstairs.

It's the sound *release.* The sound of someone emptying all that grief from their body.

"Phantom?" I ask.

"Obviously."

"Sounds like fun," Dove says. She glances at me. She has that cautiously hopeful look on her face, the way a kid might kick their feet back and forth waiting for the merry-go-round.

Her eyes say: *is it my turn yet?*

Oh. Sweet angel.

She has no idea what's coming for her.

As Dove makes small talk with Ginger and Carver, I turn my attention to the gift tree. I do a scan through the available items. There's a small, thin box tucked away in the tree. I lift the top and—yes. Exactly what I was looking for.

Discreetly, I tuck the box into my back pocket. I return to Dove, slipping my hand to the small of her back. I murmur in her ear, "Give me the tour."

She cocks her head to glance back at me. "You've already seen the club."

"Yes, but I haven't seen your version. Show me your favorite room."

Dove's fingers touch mine. She links her hand with my own.

It's hard not to see the ghosts lurking in the shadows. The memories of fuck-ups past. The last time I was here, Quinn had a way of putting her hands on me that made me feel like a crime scene. Like her fingerprints would be dusted from my body as evidence of our wrongdoings.

Dove's touch is sweetly possessive. Every part of my body feels blessed when she grazes it. It's intoxicating.

"See you later," she tells Carver and Ginger. Carver gives the head-tilt nod and then scoots in closer to Ginger, claiming his territory.

I let Dove lead. She pulls me up the staircase with the smooth, rounded wooden bannister. I follow her to the second floor, where there's a wide, studio-style space. The rigging equipment is in a heap on the floor, where it looks

like it's just been taken down. Ophelia has stopped screaming. She's in Phantom's lap now, gently sobbing as he whispers to her.

No use trying to engage them. They're in their own
world now.

Dove's fingertips guide me passed them. She takes me
into another, sectioned off room. This room is mostly empty,
save for the large, medieval-looking device in the center.
Two planks form the X of a St. Andrew's Cross.

Dove leans back against the cross, looking at me coyly.

"Is this what you want?"

She bites her lip and nods. "Mmhm."

She's smiling. She's cute. This version of Dove—this
obedient, sweet little plaything—is fucking adorable, and I'm
quickly getting addicted to it.

There's a chair in front of the cross. I take it and lace my
fingers together.

"Clothes off," I tell her. "In your bra and panties. Now."

She pops off the straps of her overalls. She pushes them
off and removes her shirt. Then she drops that too on the
floor.

"Is that how you leave your clothes?" I ask her. "In a
messy pile?"

Dove squints at me. She crouches down and folds up her
clothes neatly. Then she approaches me, holding them out. I
take them and set the pile down beside me. "Good. Back up
against the cross."

Dove goes up to the cross again. She positions herself
against it—her legs spread to match the bottom planks, her
arms outstretched above her to line up with the top planks.

God, she's a vision.

I let myself admire her. Those strong legs parted for me.
The flower tattoo that climbs her side and blooms across her
breast. The gentle curves of her body.

The rise and fall of her chest picks up in pace. I haven't even touched her yet and, already, she's panting.

She wants this. Badly.

I make her wait for it.

"Are you *sure* this is what you want?" I ask from my seat. "Because once I lock you in, I'm not going to be very nice."

She grins. "Promises, promises..."

I rise. I close the distance between us, forcing her up against the cross. "Turn around," I tell her.

She obeys. I move my hand to the soft curve of her ass. I give her a hard slap there. It draws a sudden gasp from her.

"Are you being mouthy?" I ask her.

"Yes," she says. Her voice is light, breathy.

I give her another hard smack. "Bad girl."

By which I mean: *don't stop. Don't ever stop.*

A noise that leaves her throat that is practically a purr. She's trilling.

We've barely begun, and she's already falling into sub-space.

"Christ, I'm going to have fun breaking you." I tell her. Out of the corner of my vision, I can see movement. Phantom and Ophelia have moved from their spot to watch us. Carver and Ginger have also come upstairs, and they quietly take a seat.

I take the ribbon from my pocket. I slip it around her eyes and tie it around the back of her head. "People are coming in," I inform her. "They all want to watch you scream. But you're only going to be focused on me, aren't you?"

"Yes," she says.

"New rule. When you're at my mercy, you'll address me as *sir.*"

"Yes, sir," she corrects.

Fuck. The soft, gentle way she says it makes me painfully hard.

"Face me," I tell her.

She does. Her nipples are hard knots underneath the black fabric of her bra.

I get started.

There are shackles on either end of the planks. They can slide up and down to adjust and fasten as needed. I move them to match Dove's height and then lock her into place. I clamp each ankle in. Then I fasten her wrists to the cross. She's trapped in place, spread out on the X. Exposed to my whims.

"How does that feel?" I ask her.

She tries to move her arms. She can't—the shackles are too tight. "Good," she replies.

I crook my finger. Slowly, I graze it down her side. I trace the curve of her body from her breast down to her hip. She shivers and pushes against her restraints, hunting for my touch.

I pet a slow, lazy line over the center of her body. "Will you tell me what you like?"

Her lips thin. She presses them together thoughtfully, then says, "I used to know. Now…I'm not so sure."

"We'll figure it out together."

I remove the box from my back pocket and open it up. A Wartenberg wheel rests in the cushion inside. It's not unlike the one she used on me the first night we played together—a stainless steel rod with a wheel at the end covered in tiny, pointy spikes.

She can't see me. She has no idea what's coming. But she's twitching with anticipation.

I get off on tormenting her like this.

"Should we play a guessing game?" I ask her. "What do you think I took from the tree?"

"Um." Her voice is alight with curiosity. "A paddle?"

"I'll give you a clue. It's a classic. A tried-and-true favorite."

"A flogger?"

"I'm going to touch you with it. Do you trust me?"

She nods blindly. "Yes, sir." The way she says *sir* feels like a prayer.

I touch the spike very lightly to the bare skin under her breasts. She's hyper-sensitive and even the small brush of spikes makes her entire body jerk in place.

"Oh," she gasps. "It's sharp."

I slowly roll it down the center of her body. Down her navel, to the rim of her panties. She tries to squirm, but she can't. She's locked too tightly in place.

She whines, "it hurts."

"Poor thing." I press in harder. She whimpers. I move my lips to the curve of her ear. "I'm not hearing any guesses."

"It's—um—oh! It's a wheel. A…fuck…"

"A fuck?" I move the wheel to the sensitive skin of her inner thigh. I run it up so it nearly grazes her cunt.

She gasps. She jerks upwards, but she's trapped in place. Her mouth works, hunting for the right words, and she finally finds them:

"A Wartenberg wheel! It's a Wartenberg wheel."

"There she is." I pull the wheel back. It's left a line of tiny red pinpricks on her skin. I lower myself in front of her. I press my lips to the angry dots. The muscles in her abdomen tense and clench as I draw kisses below her little bellybutton. Up her thigh. She's wearing black, but I can tell she's soaked through. The thick scent of her arousal has my head spinning.

The tables have turned. Her desperation is delicious.

She's making soft, whimpery noises. She's lost, deep in sub-space. I doubt it even registers that she's amassed a small crowd. She's focused solely on me. The way I pleasure her. The way I hurt her.

I straighten up. I slip my fingers through her hair, grab a rough handful, and pin her head back against the cross.

"How's are you feeling, boss?"

I want to remind her: no matter how helpless she is, she's still in charge.

I'll take her sanity. I'll make her helpless. I'll degrade her and I'll hurt her—exactly how she wants it.

But I'll never take her power away from her.

She tilts her head into my grip. Wanting. Her hips give a small roll against her binds. "I feel like every single nerve is on fire."

"Good." I brush my lips over hers. "Now. Let's play."

THE END

NOTE FROM ADORA

Thank you for reading Whimper Wonderland!

I poured my entire heart into Dove and Dorian's unconventional, kinky love story. If you enjoyed reading, help other readers find it and **please consider leaving a review** — it means so much to hear what you think.

You can also preorder The Seekers Club Book #2, which features a new couple, but will have some veeeery familiar faces in it...

If you want to live in this world a little longer, you can find bonus content such as...

- **Spotify playlist** & aesthetic board
- **Extended epilogue** of their St. Andrew's Cross scene

Book #2 ➡️ https://geni.us/seekersclub2
Bonus content ➡️ https://adoracrooksbooks.com/whimper-wonderland/

ABOUT THE AUTHOR

USA Today bestselling author Adora Crooks writes romance with heart, humor, and heat. She is a sucker for kick-ass heroines and the strong, brooding men who crave them (and sometimes crave each other, too).

A former New Yorker, she currently resides in the magical city of New Orleans with her beloved and their two nutty mutts. Adora lives off of coffee, cookies, and book reviews and daydreams about dirty romances with happy-ever-afters.

Join Adora's newsletter to download a free romance 
https://adoracrooksbooks.com/gift